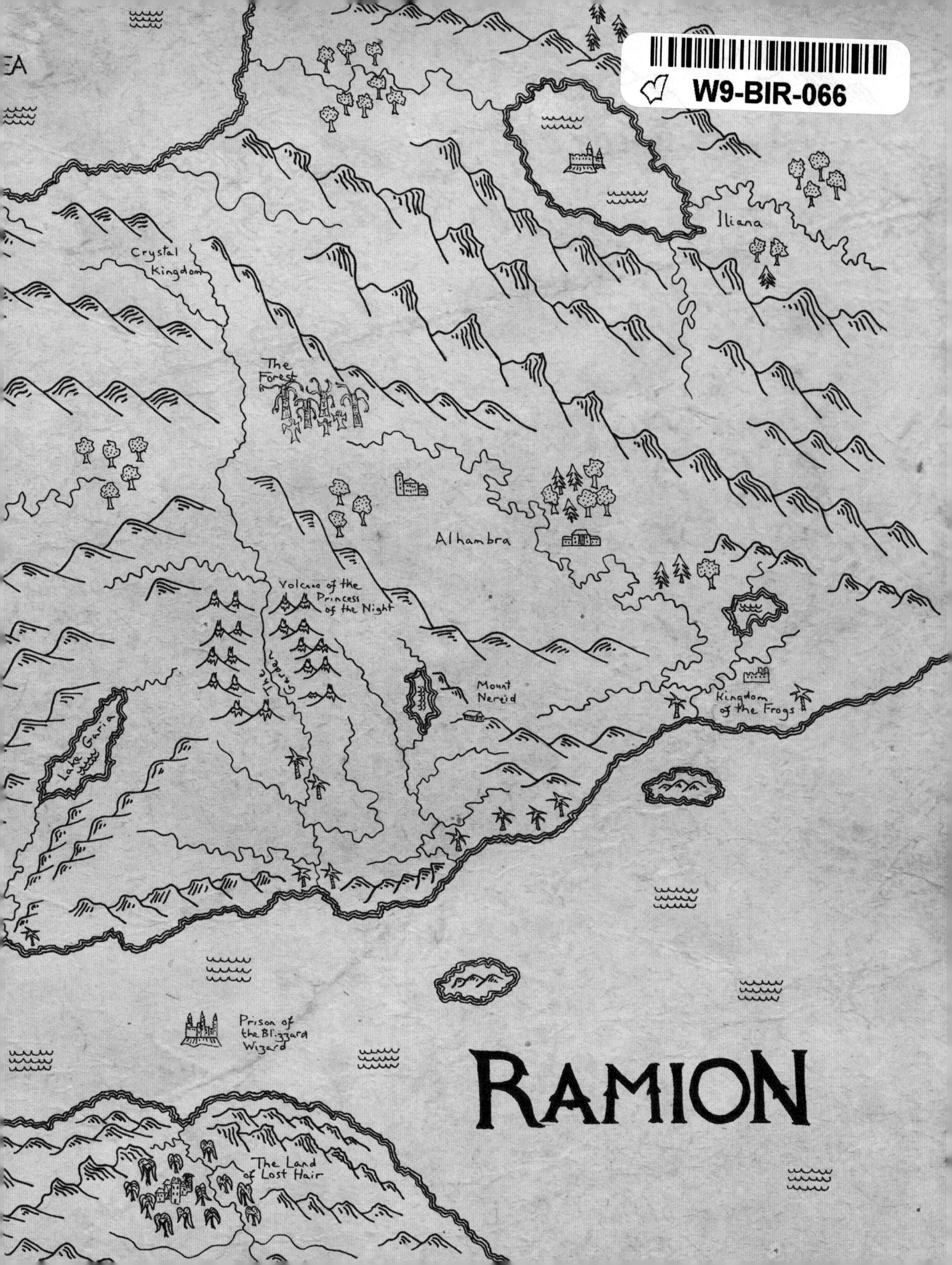
Crystal Kingdom
Iliana
The Forest
Alhambra
Volcano of the Princess of the Night
Mount Nereid
Kingdom of the Frogs
Lake Garia
Prison of the Blizzard Wizard
The Land of Lost Hair
RAMION

THE
BODY COLLECTOR

Published by

Perronet Press

www.ramion-books.com

Copyright © Text and illustrations

Frank Hinks 2019

A CIP record for this book is available from the British Library

ISBN: 9781909938205

Printed in China by CP Printing Ltd.
Layout by Jennifer Stephens
Font designer - Bajo La Luna Producciones

TALES OF RAMION
THE
BODY COLLECTOR

FRANK HINKS

Perronet

2019

TALES of RAMION

THE GARDENER

*Lord of Ramion, guardian
and protector*

THE GUIDE

*Friend and servant of the
Gardener*

SNUGGLE

*Dream Lord sent to protect the
boys from the witch Griselda*

SCROOEY-LOOEY

*Greedy, rude, half-mad rabbit,
a friend of the boys*

TILNEY

*The most precious of plants,
can reverse evil magic*

GLORIA

*Vegetarian eagle,
wife of hen-pecked Archibald*

JULIUS
ALEXANDER
BENJAMIN

Three brothers who long for adventure

THE BOYS' FATHER

*Loves rock and roll,
very keen on dancing*

THE BOYS MOTHER

*Has a very loud voice, not unlike
that of Griselda*

GRISELDA THE GRUNCH

A witch who longs to eat the boys

THE DIM DAFT DWARVES

Julioso, Aliano, Benjio, Griselda's guards

BORIS

Griselda's pet skull, strangely fond of her

GLOBEROUS GHOSTS

The fattest, ooziest ghosts that have ever lived

MYSTIC MUMMIES

Cannot stand children who pick their noses

VENOMOUS VAMPIRES

Very snooty, only want to drink your blood

THE MINI SKULLS

*Nip. Nit, Nik, Nix and Nib,
so evil they will eat you*

THE BODY COLLECTOR

Charlie Stench, not a nice man

SCARY SCOTS

*Five minutes of their sound
and a child will explode*

CHAPTER ONE

After the witch Griselda and Boris her pet skull got back from the Kingdom of the Deep the atmosphere in the remains of Grunch Castle was not happy. Griselda stormed from room to room slamming doors, kicking dwarves and howling like a banshee, "Damn and blast that useless skull! Would not even fry a swordfish! What a wimp! Completely useless!" The dim daft dwarves (Julioso, Aliano and Benjio) slunk around like frightened shadows expecting every moment to be kicked.

Boris did his best to keep out of Griselda's way, hiding on a shelf in the dwarves' shed at the back of the ruined tower dreaming gloomily of golden sandy beaches and beautiful girls in bikinis, murmuring softly to himself, "I wish I had a body. It's no fun being a skull. How I long to dance and swim!"

Then early one morning the rising sun shone through the dusty window of the shed, and searched out Boris, shining brightly into his blinking eyes. Roused from his gloomy sleep he had a sudden picture of himself as he had been before he became a skull (whether a vision, dream or distant memory he was not sure). He was a builder, young (well, not much more than thirty), good looking (well, not ugly). He was visiting Stench Manor to repair the roof of the kitchen porch. He set his ladders against the wall, was just about to clamber up, when a fat man with bald shining head and bulbous eyes came out and offered him a drink to quench his thirst. He drank and everything went black.

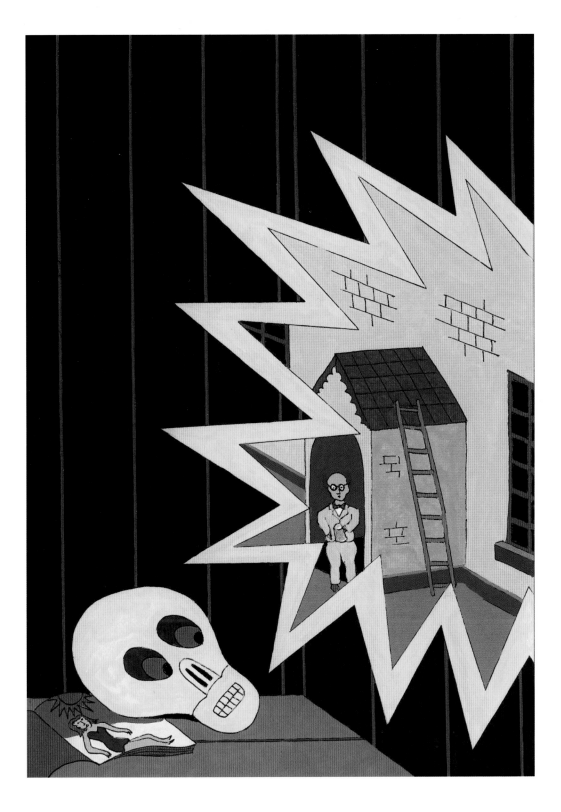

Boris suddenly cried out, "That must have been when I lost my body. I wonder if I could persuade Griselda to get it back." At the thought that perhaps one day he would get back his body he began to whistle softly. He no longer felt gloomy. He felt like having fun. "I'll go out into the forest and see if I can play some tricks."

Later that day, when Boris returned to the tower, he was whistling loudly, and clearly pleased with himself. "Boris come here!" Griselda screeched at her pet skull. "I need cheering up. Have you done anything evil to walkers in the forest?" Boris floated excitedly to Griselda. He hoped she would cradle him in her arms and scratch his bony head, but she just glared at him, hands on hips, and howled, "Evil! Evil! Evil! I hope this time someone really did get hurt."

"Oh mistress! Mistress!" hissed Boris more than a little worried. "I was floating through the forest when I spied a group of ramblers eating their packed lunch. As the leader of the group raised a cup of tea to his lips I floated out of the bushes, flashed my sockets, gnashed my gnashers and cleared my throat."

"What happened next?" asked Griselda with a sneering laugh.

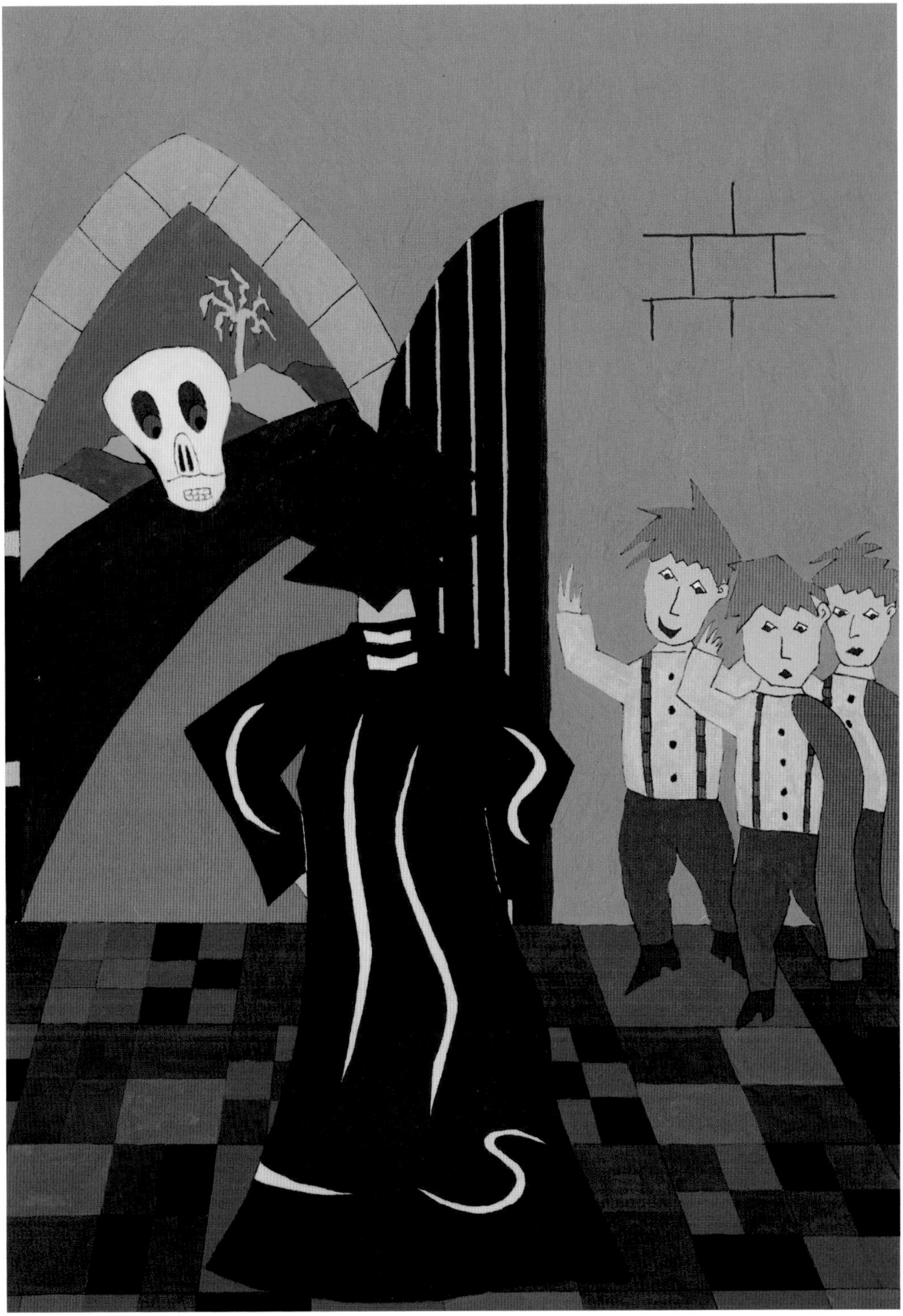

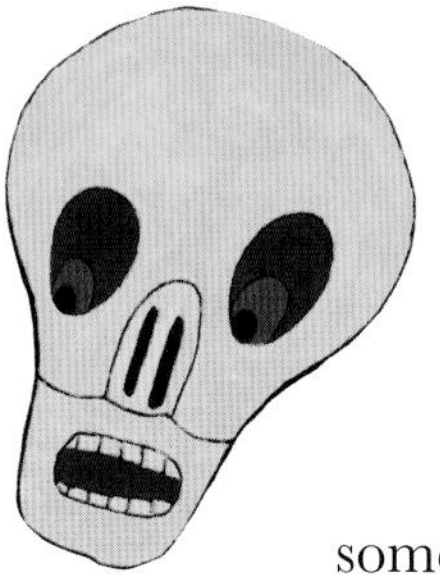

"In surprise he poured the tea down the back of a man standing beside him."

"Was the man badly scalded?" asked Griselda with longing.

"Oh no mistress!" hissed Boris, shocked at the idea that someone might have got hurt. "I would not have done it if the tea had been boiling hot."

"Shame."

"But the shock of having tea poured down his back was so great he squeezed the jam out of his doughnut over the heads of three ladies sitting on the ground. They screamed. I could not help laughing. So I gave them a quick flash with my red sockets. They screamed again. Then I got out my gnashers and gnashed behind their bottoms. They screamed again. Then they all ran off leaving the lunch which I chomped up with my gnashers."

"Pathetic! Absolutely pathetic!" shrieked Griselda picking up her magic staff and sending a thunderflash which echoed in the bony skull.

"Oh mistress! There was no need for that."

"No need! No need! You should go out into the forest to do evil, not play silly tricks. I have had enough. You're useless. I shall get a new skull – someone young, strong and evil."

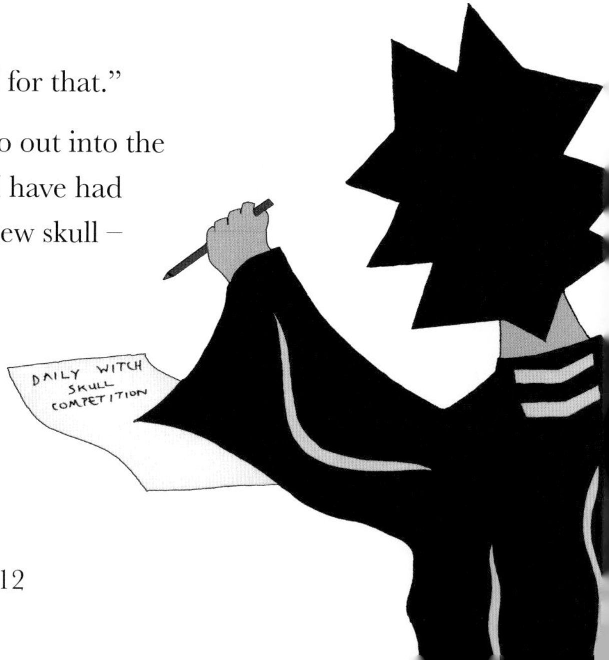
DAILY WITCH
SKULL
COMPETITION

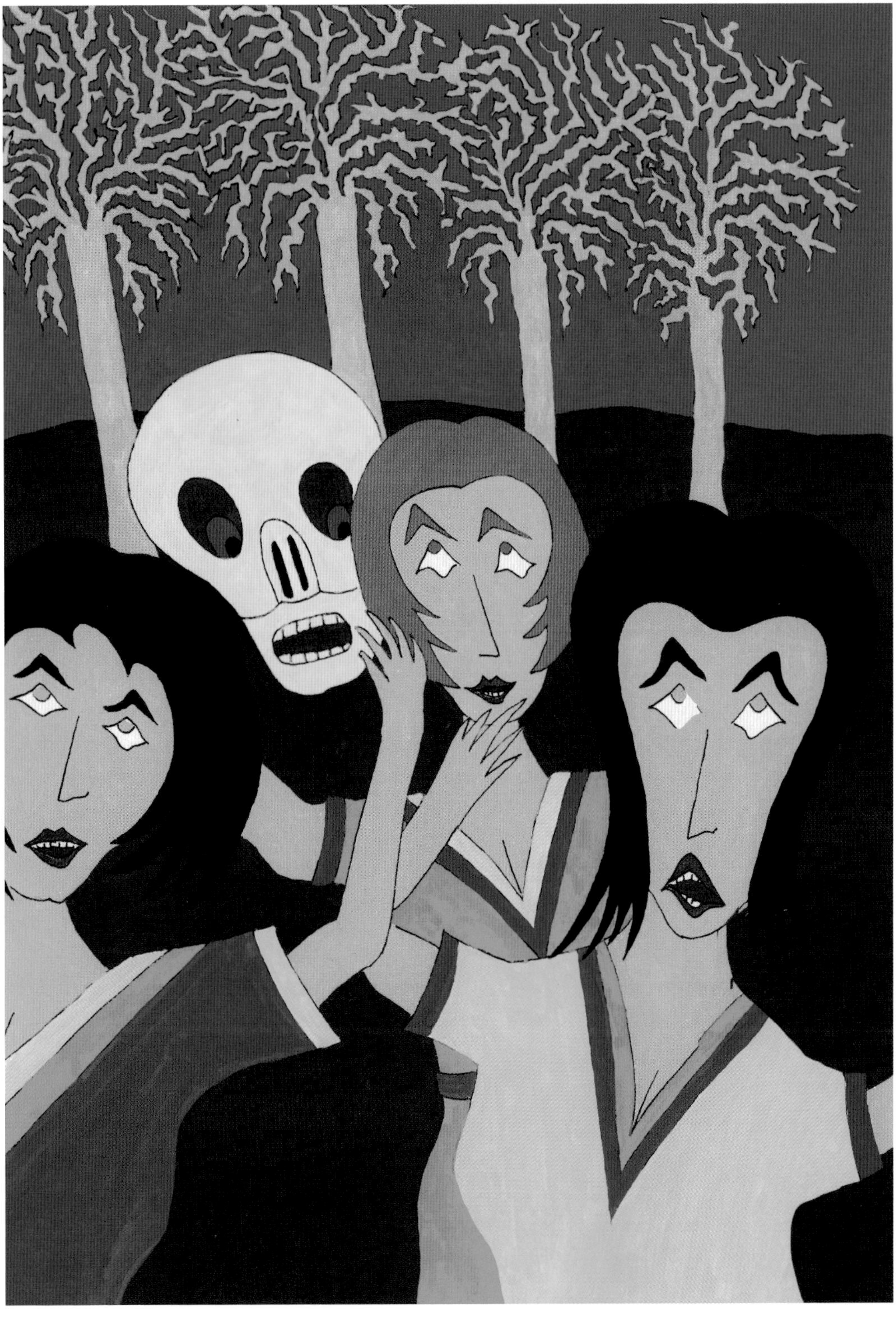

"Mistress! No! I l-o-v-e you."

"Shut up Boris! Don't be so soppy. You are simply not evil enough. You will have to go. But only when I have got a replacement. Until then you will do as I command."

"But of course," nodded Boris, sadly realising that he would never be able to persuade Griselda to get back his body.

Griselda walked over to her desk and took some papers out of a drawer. "I have been collecting tokens from the Daily Witch. There is a competition with a choice of first prize: either a skull or mystery box of evil. I was going to choose a mystery box of evil, but you're so hopeless I shall tick the box for a skull instead."

Griselda got out a pencil, ticked the box for a skull, then answered the questions in the competition. "What do you do with a skull who ceases to do evil?" "Grind him up and use him as bonemeal," muttered Griselda, writing furiously.

Suddenly Boris had a thought and began to look more cheerful. "Mistress! Perhaps you will not win. Then you will keep me."

Griselda looked at Boris: a hard look of contempt. "I will not leave winning to chance. With this spell I cannot lose."

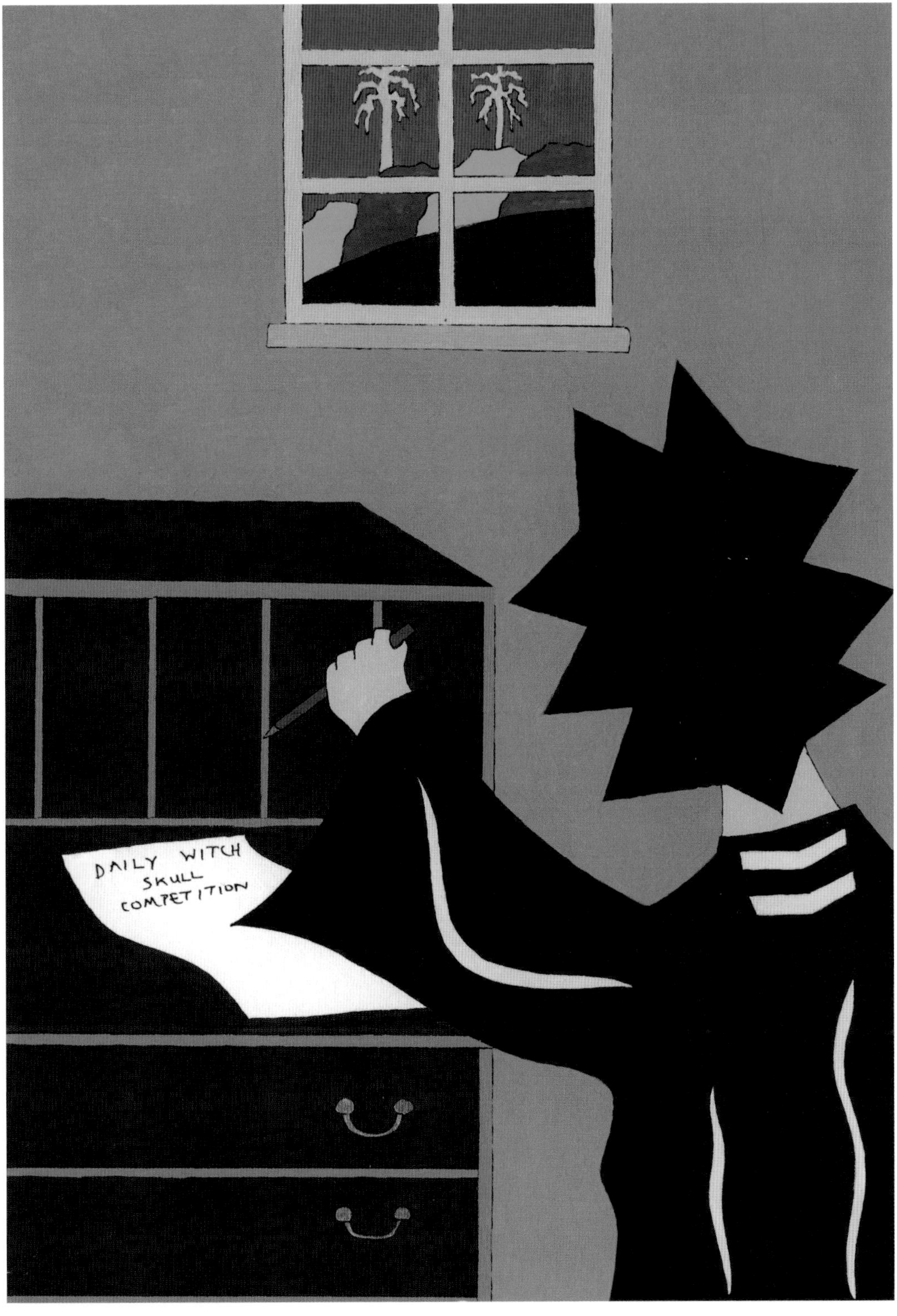
DAILY WITCH
SKULL
COMPETITION

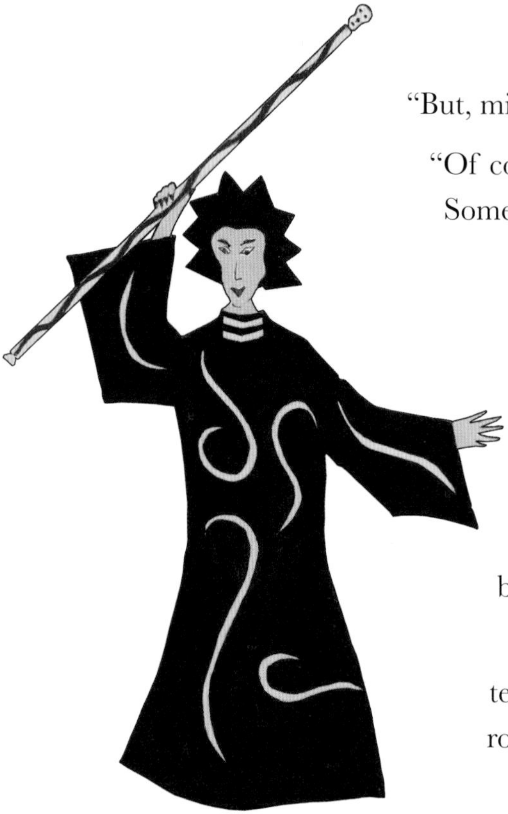

"But, mistress, that's cheating!"

"Of course it's cheating. I'm a witch. Sometimes, Boris, I think you're stupid."

So saying Griselda raised her magic staff and muttered words of magic. In a blinding flash the competition form and tokens jumped into the envelope which addressed and sealed itself. "Now take this to the post: if you fail to post it, I shall grind you into little bits."

Sadly Boris picked up the letter in his teeth and floated off towards the post, tears rolling from his eye sockets.

"She doesn't love me. She'll never get back my body. She'll kick me out as soon as she gets some new young skull to take my place."

In pain Boris banged himself against a tree. Then he had an idea. Swiftly he used laser beams from his eye sockets to turn the teardrops into steam. He steamed open the letter, rubbed out the tick for a new skull, ticked the box for a mystery box of evil, resealed the letter and whistling cheerfully through his front teeth, floated off to the post box in Romney Street.

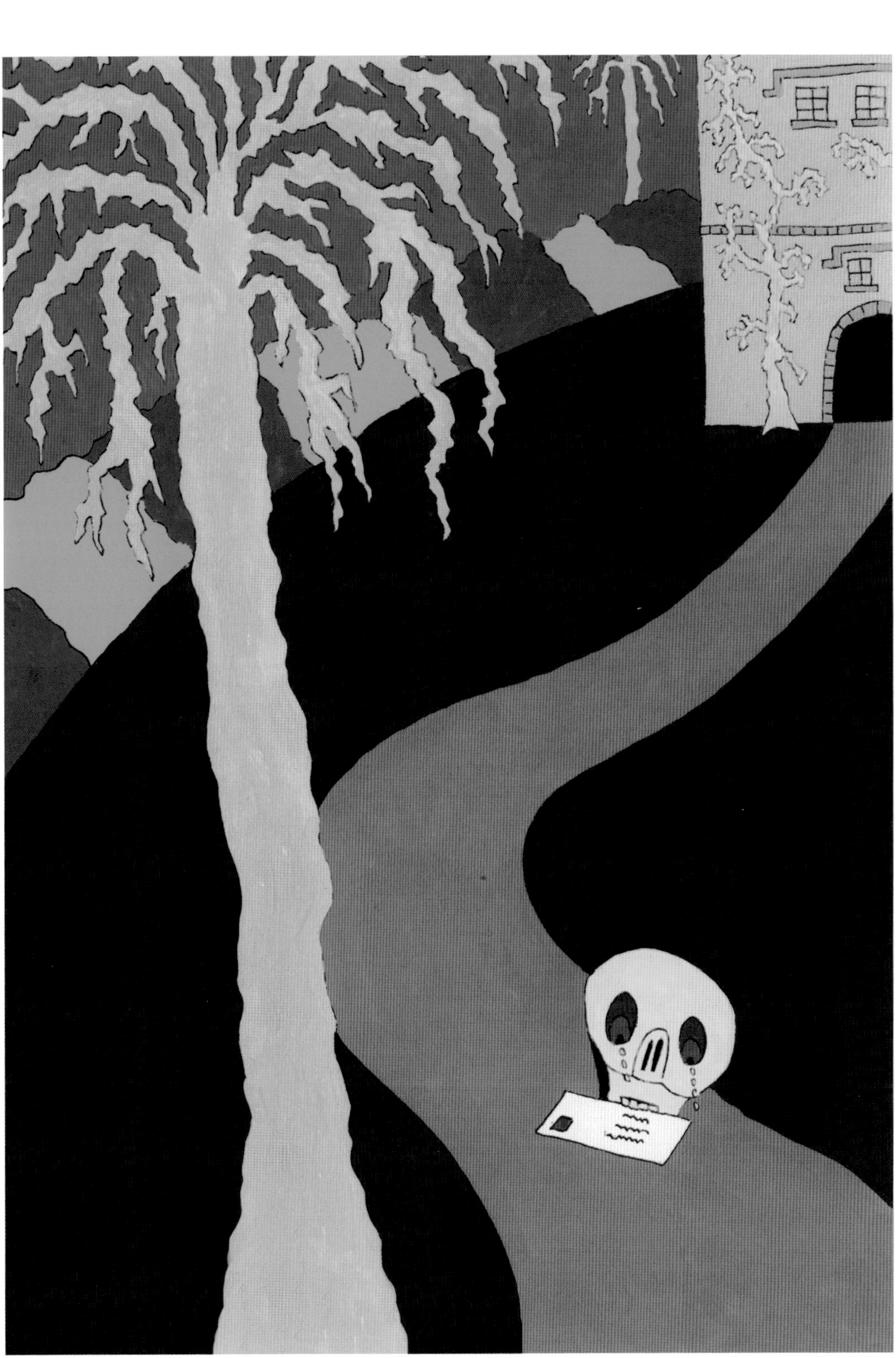

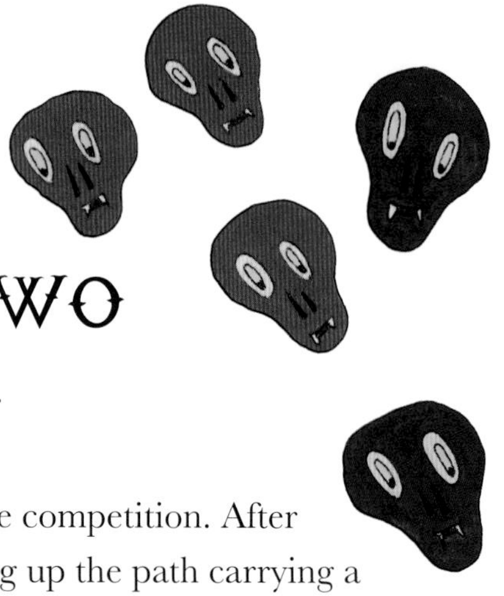

Chapter Two

Griselda waited anxiously for the results of the competition. After several weeks she saw the postman struggling up the path carrying a heavy box sealed in black and bearing labels: "Mystery Box of Evil. Handle with care." She ran to meet him (he turned and fled). When she saw that it was not a new young skull, but a mystery box of evil she roared in fury, "Boris come here!" Nervously the skull floated to her. "You changed the competition form, did you not?" she cried, raising her magic staff and sending a triple thunderflash which pinned Boris to the ground.

Then Griselda jumped up and down on Boris. "Ow! Ow! Ow! Mistress, stop it!" he yelped, as her leather boots drove him deeper and deeper into the earth.

After the skull had almost disappeared beneath the surface Griselda turned to the sealed box. She tore open a letter which read: "You have won First Prize, a Mystery Box of Evil." She threw the letter to one side, ignoring the warning in big black letters "Beware the Mini-Skulls: keep them under lock and key. They are so evil they may even try to eat you."

Griselda tore off the wrapping. "What have we here?" she cried, as she lifted the lid of the box and peered inside. Out floated five Globerous Ghosts, five Mystic Mummies, five Venomous Vampires and five Scary Scots playing bagpipes. "What a dreadful noise!" Griselda screamed, as she peered inside the box.

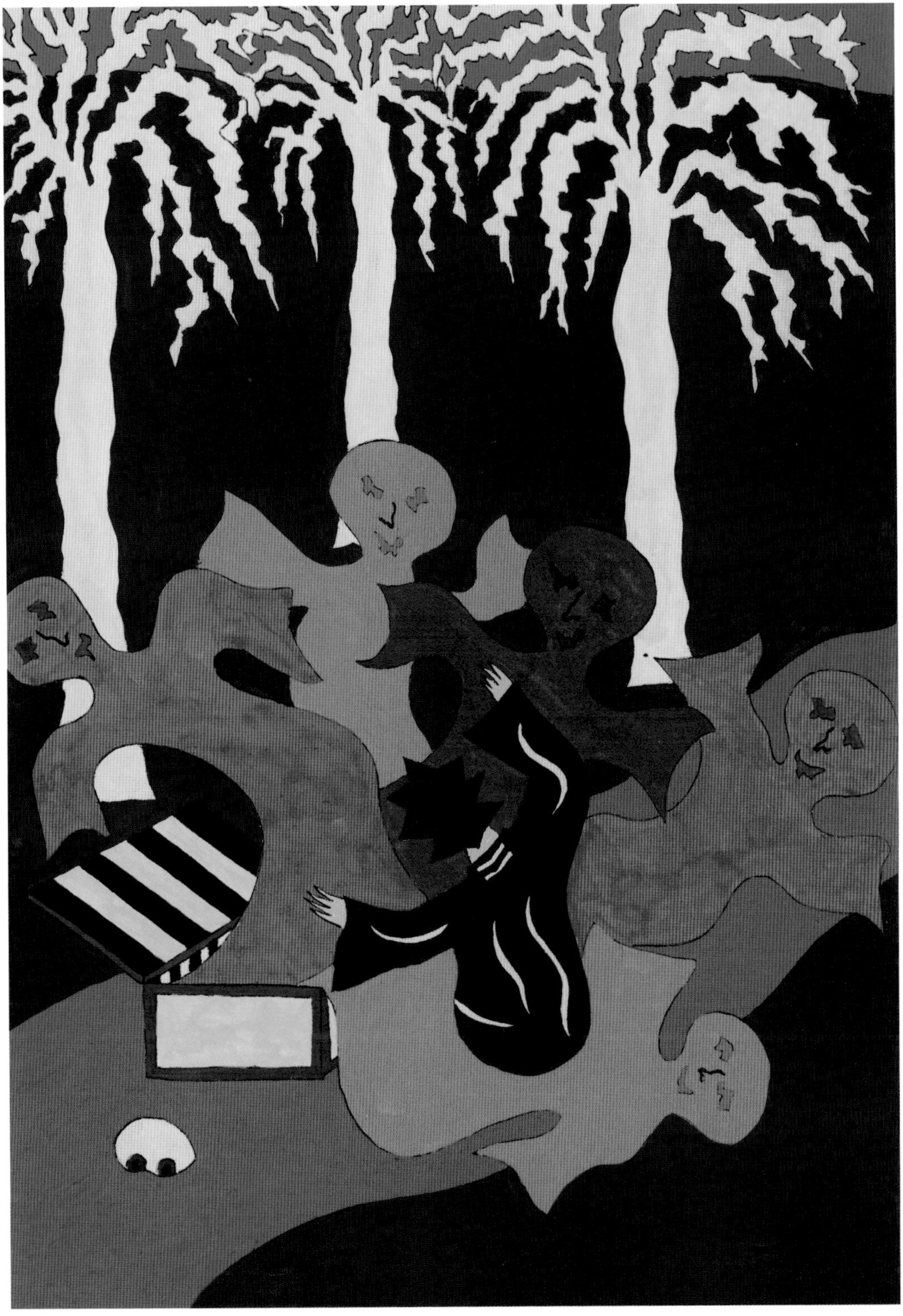

At the bottom was a metal grill. Beneath it five mini-skulls, Nip, Nit, Nik, Nix and Nib, looked up at Griselda, grinning inanely. "Toy boys!" yelled Griselda in triumph as she unlocked the grill and let them out.

"Mistress no!" cried Boris who had struggled out of the path, and was reading the warning in the letter. "They are so evil they will destroy you!"

"Shut up Boris! I know you. You're jealous. With five young skulls about the castle I've no more use for an aged has-been like you. Get out of here."

So saying Griselda lifted her foot and kicked Boris deep into the forest. As she was busy kicking Boris, laser beams leapt out of the eye sockets of the mini-skulls: they burnt the warning letter.

"My dears!" purred Griselda in delight. "I am so glad you are full of fire. Come, join me in the tower, but first I must get rid of these monsters." (The noise from the Scary Scots was absolutely dreadful.) Swiftly she told them the way to The Old Vicarage. "Destroy the boys, cat and rabbit. I would like to eat the boys but, because they are guarded by Snuggle, something always goes wrong."

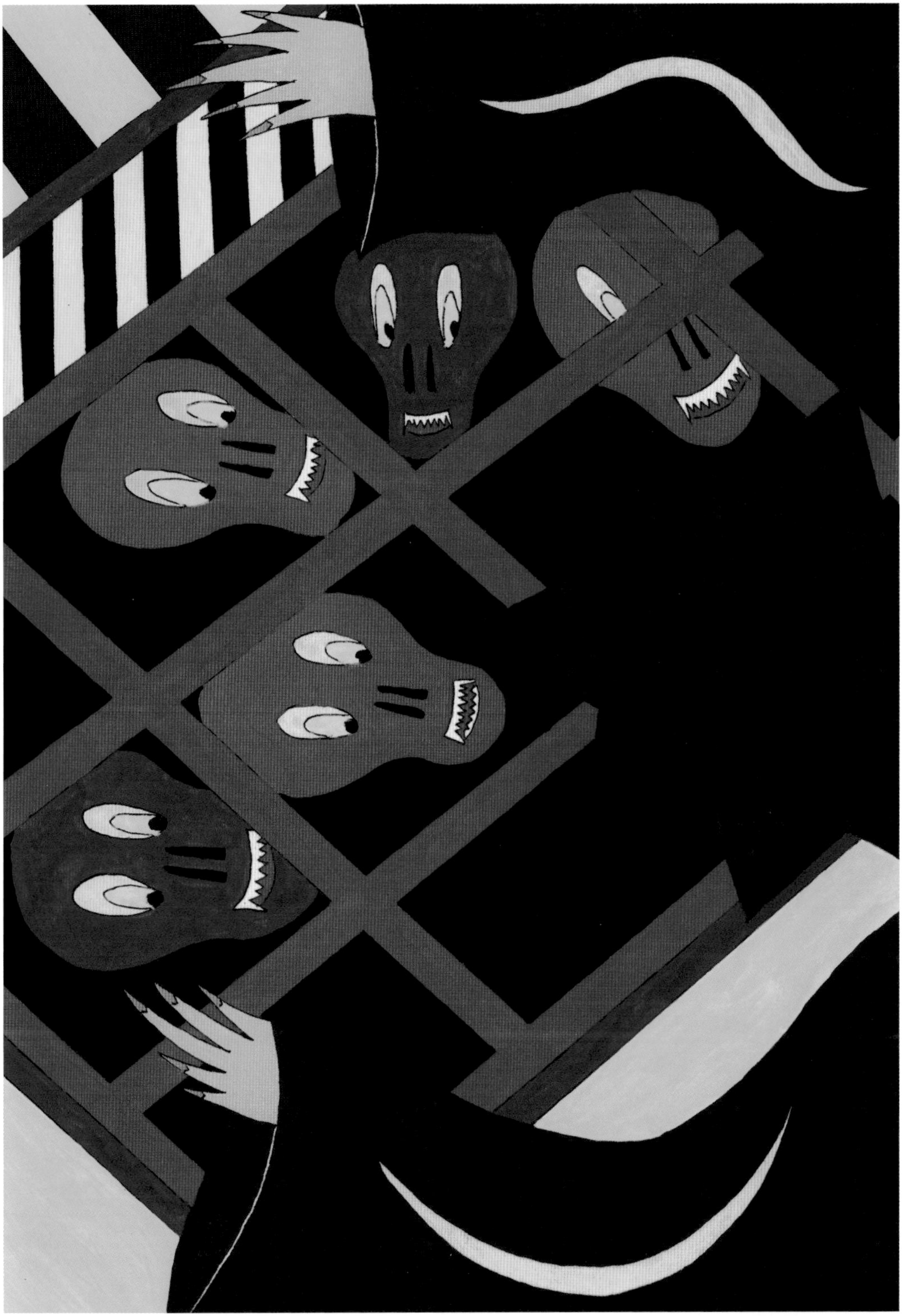

As the five mini-skulls followed Griselda into
the tower the dim daft dwarves shook with terror.
"What horrid teeth!" "What flaming eye sockets!"
"They're bound to get us." "Let's go and find Boris."
Gloomily they trudged off into the forest and found
Boris deep inside a bush.

Boris was talking to himself. "I love her madly.
Now she has five young skulls she'll never want me.
I'll never get my body back."

"Cheer up, Boris!" cried the dim daft dwarves. "If
Griselda does not want you in the tower, you can still
live in the shed with us."

Boris did not reply, but continued to murmur to himself, "I
love her, but she doesn't want me."

The dim daft dwarves picked Boris up, carried him home to their
shed, and put him on a shelf. They did their best to cheer him up. They
even went and found his favourite holiday brochures (with young women
sunbathing on beaches in the south of France) but he ignored them, turned
towards the wall and muttered softly, "She doesn't l-o-v-e me. Now she
never will."

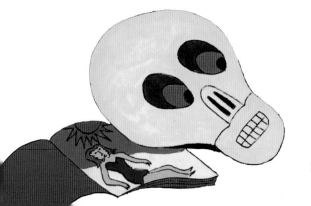

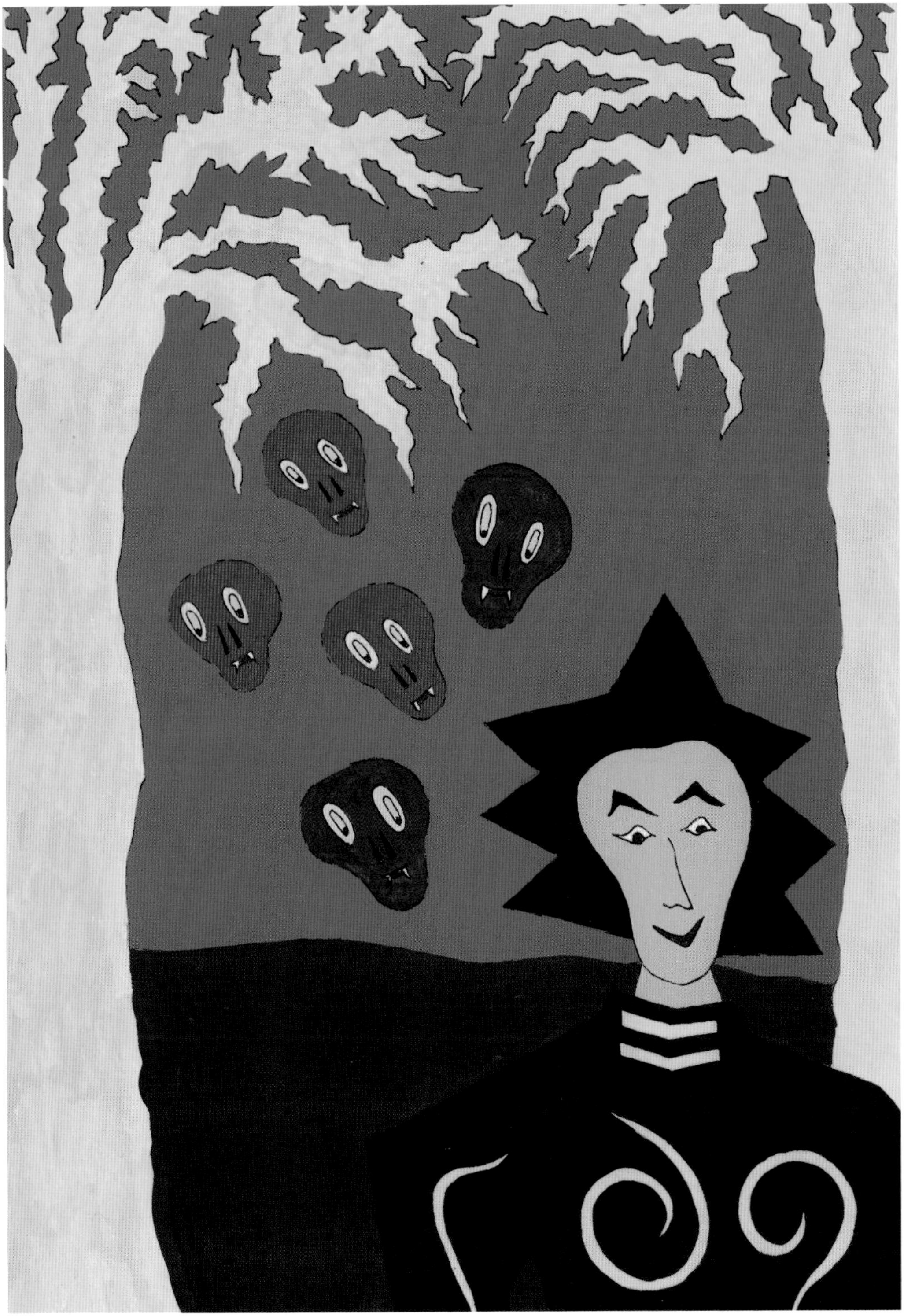

CHAPTER THREE

Julius, Alexander and Benjamin were playing on the trampoline at the bottom of the garden. Scrooey-Looey was lying underneath chewing a carrot. Silently four Globerous Ghosts floated above the gate to the churchyard, beneath the ancient box tree, across the upper lawn. The boys were bouncing in the air, twisting and turning upside down when the Globerous Ghosts leapt up to get them (a single touch from their outstretched arms would turn a boy or rabbit into a ghostly glob). "Oh help!" shrieked Scrooey-Looey, choking on a carrot.

But after their adventure with the Blizzard Wizard the boys had been practising. Without a second thought they stuck out their tongues, and the Globerous Ghosts exploded into a thousand ghostly globs, which splattered all around the garden.

"Clear up that mess!" shouted their father from the kitchen, as he turned his back on the garden, and bent down to fill the dishwasher.

At that moment five Mystic Mummies crept round the outside of the garage and approaching the trampoline from the other side, swiftly stretched out to turn the boys and rabbit into piles of dust.

"Oh no you don't!" shouted the boys as, jumping higher out of reach, they turned upside down and picked their noses.

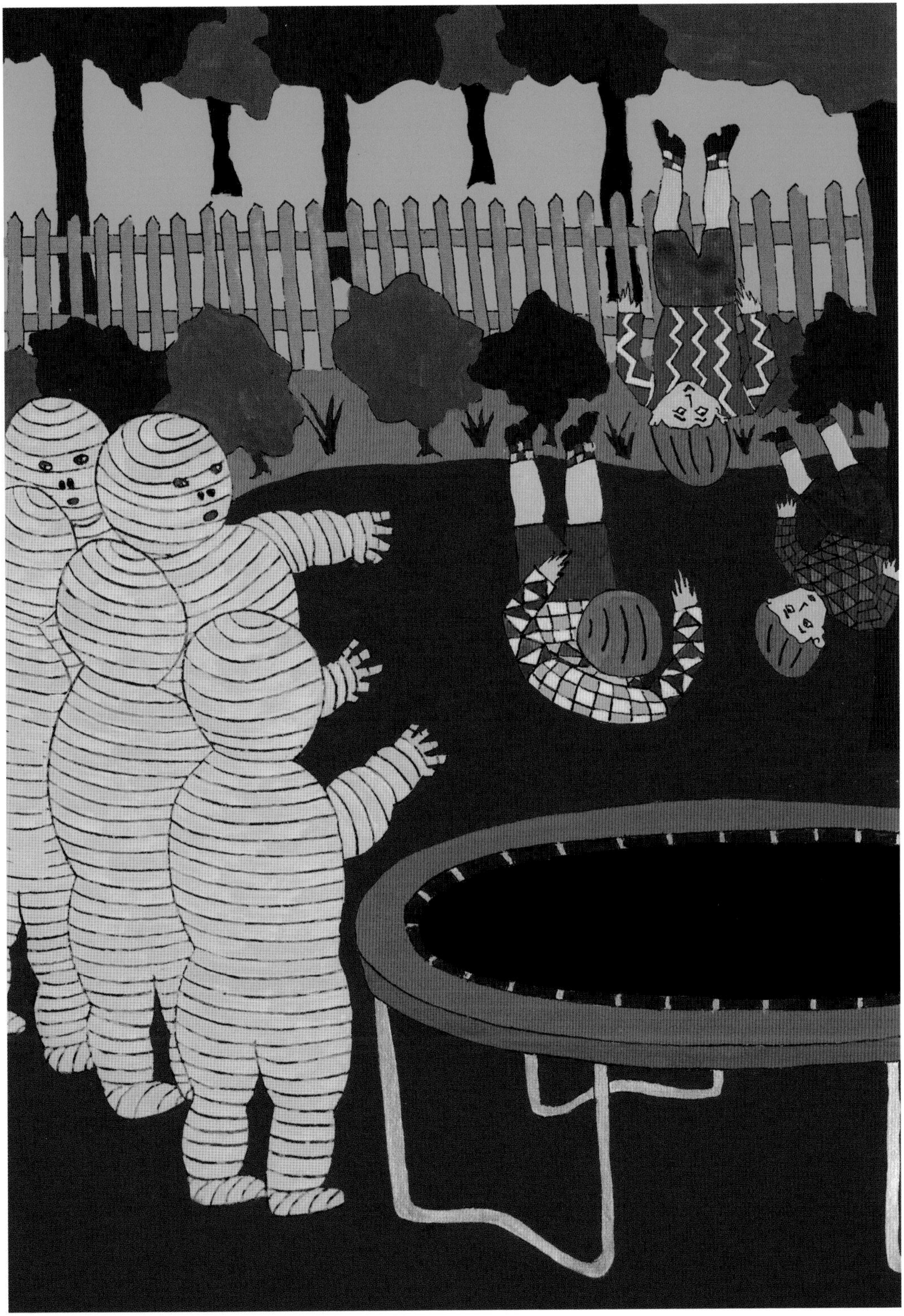

"Germs! Germs!" howled the Mystic Mummies, as their bandages unravelled and their innards turned to dust.

"Well done!" squeaked Scrooey-Looey, stuffing another carrot into his mouth.

Then five Venomous Vampires leapt over The Old Vicarage fence and strode towards the trampoline, "Come here, boys. We only want your blood."

"Not likely!" cried the boys as with triple somersaults, they leapt off the trampoline, landed in the dahlia bed, stuck their hands in the earth, and held them out towards the Venomous Vampires.

"Oh no! Not the muddy hands!" exclaimed the Venomous Vampires, as their heads shot off and bounced away, and their bodies ran off to the dry cleaners.

"Get off the flower bed!" shouted the boys' father from the kitchen as he turned once more to fill the dishwasher.

Swiftly the boys scrambled out of the dahlia bed and back onto the trampoline. "Great! Great! Great!" they shouted bouncing higher and higher into the air. "We really got them."

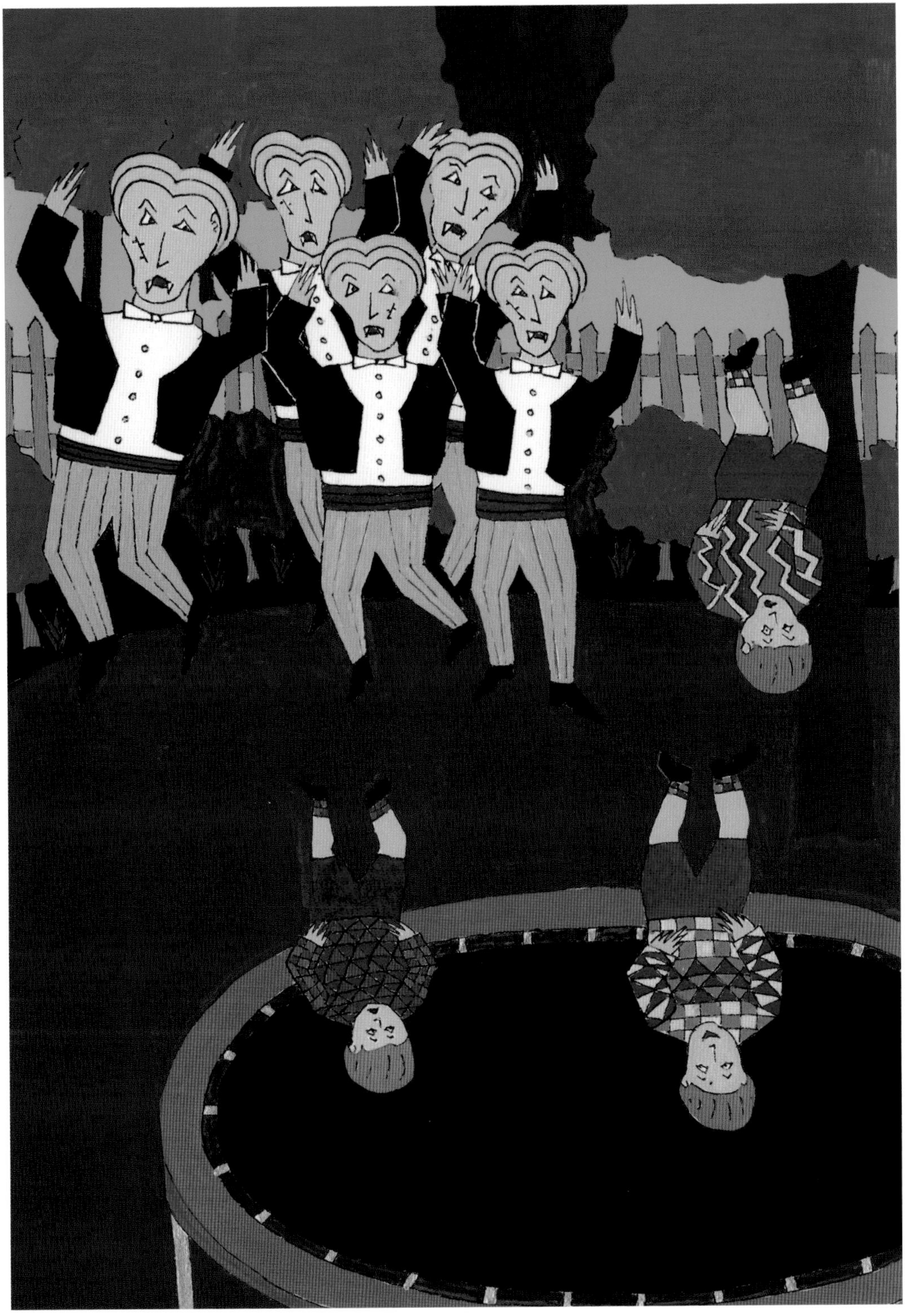

But at that moment five Scary Scots playing bagpipes marched down the road, up the driveway, across the lawn, and surrounded the trampoline.

"Oh help!" squeaked Scrooey-Looey, choking on another carrot.

The bagpipes wheezed and groaned. The noise was ghastly. Five minutes of that sound and a boy (or rabbit) will explode. The boys hugged each other in terror.

"We don't know how to defeat Scary Scots."

"And there aren't any Hero Hedgehogs."

"Not in Shoreham."

The five minutes was nearly up when Snuggle came running. Swiftly he unsheathed his claws, and as he slashed the bagpipes the Scary Scots soared through the air like burst balloons. One disappeared over the church tower, two over the roof of The Old Vicarage, and the last two bounced off the roof of a disused grain store.

"Hurrah! Hurrah!" shouted the boys jumping up and down. "Well done Snuggle! We've got them! Got them! Got them! Got them!"

The boys' mother came running up the garden. Her face was black. Her voice roared like a clap of thunder. "Be quiet! Be quiet! Never in all my days have I heard children make such noise. You've disturbed the whole village."

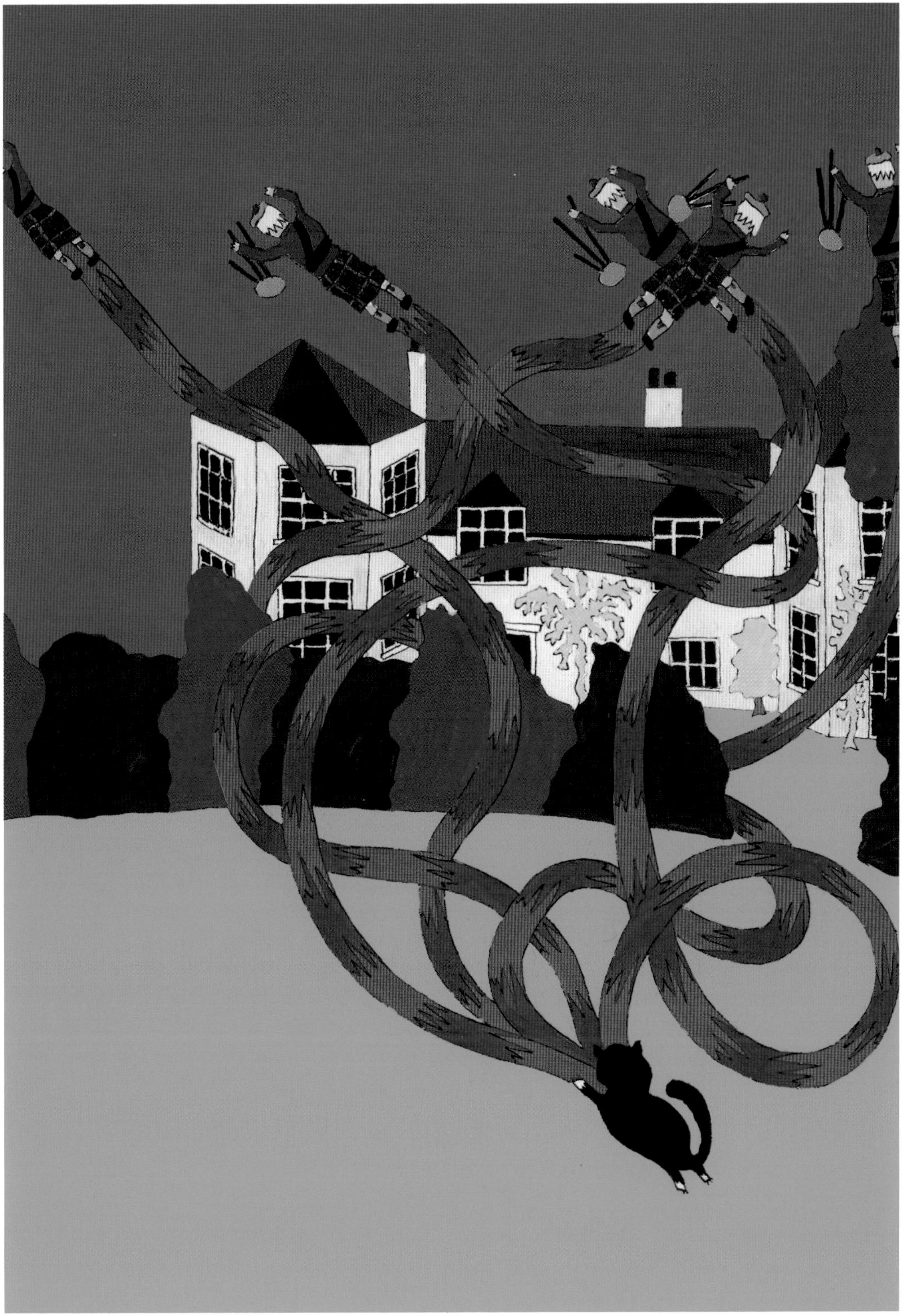

"But Mum it wasn't us," started Benjamin.

"Sssh!" whispered Julius. "It's no good telling her it was Scary Scots."

"She'll say we're lying," added Alexander.

"What was that, Benjamin?"

"Nothing Mum."

"You're all covered in mud – your hands are dreadful. A bath, then bed. Julius run the bath."

The boys ran into the house and up the stairs. As they ran Alexander whispered to his brothers, "Snuggle once said that monsters hunt in packs of five. There were only four Globerous Ghosts. We must be careful."

As Benjamin and Alexander began to get undressed, Julius went into the nursery bathroom, bending over the bath to put in the plug. As he bent down a Globerous Ghost squeezed out of the plughole, and soared up to get him. Quick as a flash Julius jumped backwards, head over heels. As he did so he stuck out his tongue.

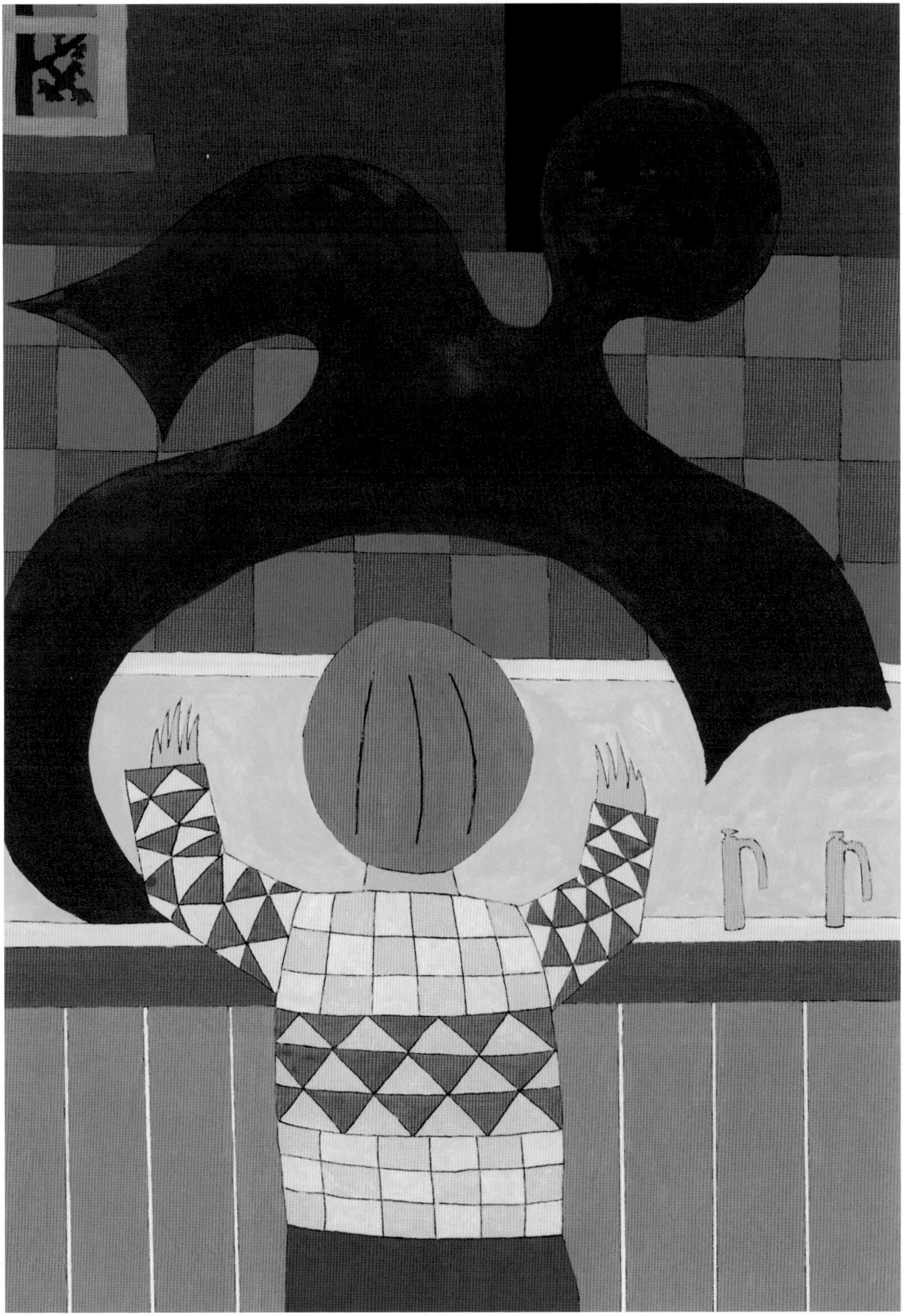

The Globerous Ghost exploded into a thousand ghostly globs which splattered all around the bathroom. "Oh no!" groaned Julius. "What a mess. Mum will be furious."

When the boys' mother saw gunge dripping down the walls of the bathroom, she was not pleased. In fact she was so cross that she went to fetch the boys' father. When he saw gunge dripping down the bathroom walls, he was very cross indeed.

"But, Dad it wasn't us," insisted Benjamin.

"Who was it then? Mr Nobody?"

"It was a ghost," replied Benjamin.

"Benje, be quiet – they won't believe us," hissed his brothers.

Benjamin continued firmly, "It was a Globerous Ghost. Julius defeated it by sticking out his tongue and it exploded all over the bathroom."

"What utter utter nonsense!" shouted their Dad. "You trash the bathroom and then tell a pack of lies. No supper for you. Go straight to bed."

Benjamin slammed the bedroom door behind him. He was in a state of rebellion. "I was only telling the truth. Unfair! Unfair! Unfair!"

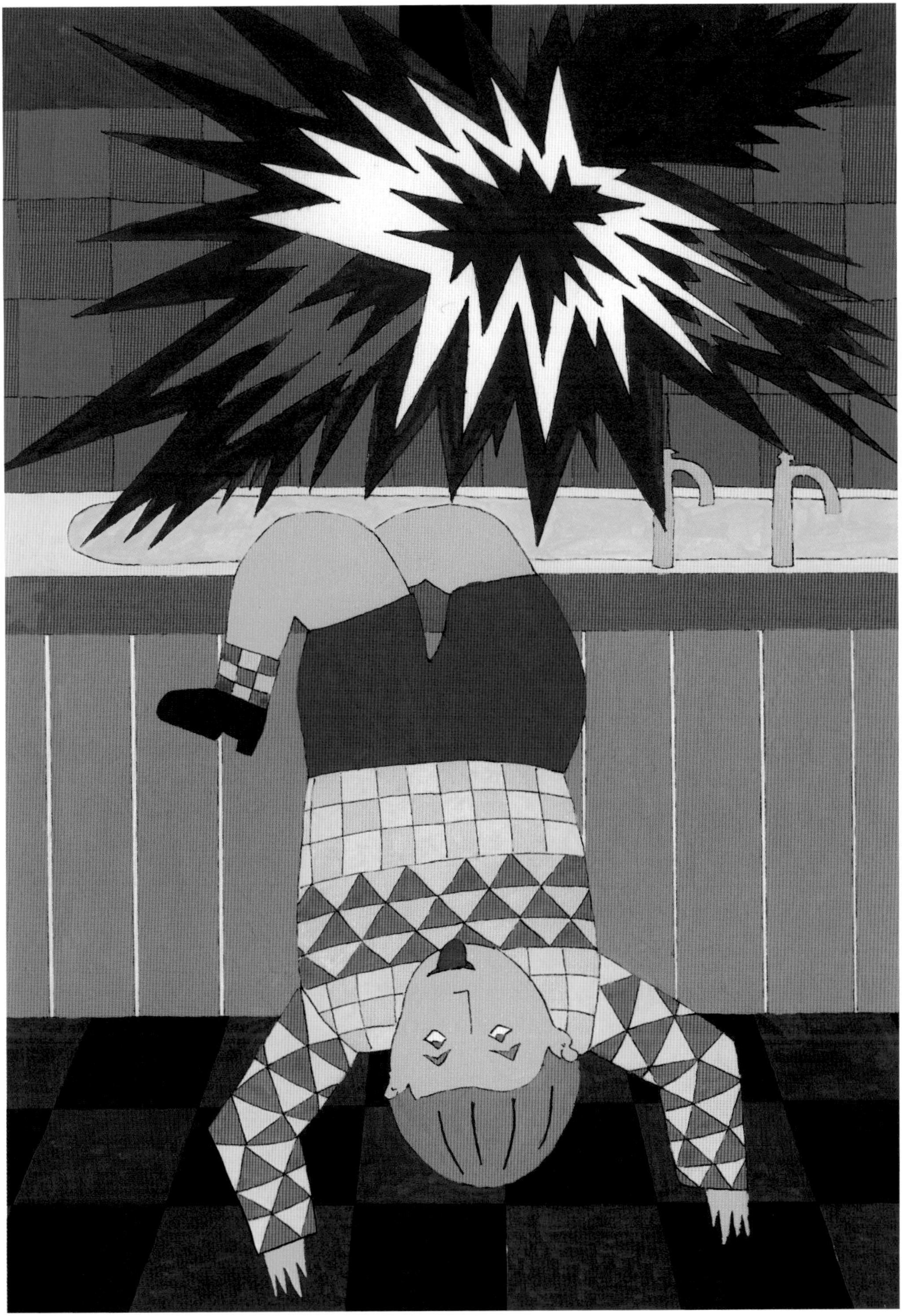

Chapter Four

Boris lay upon the shelf moaning softly, "I l-o-v-e her deeply, but she doesn't want me." His thoughts became more and more gloomy. "She never liked me. She always sends thunderflashes which echo in my bony skull and kicks me out the window. Just because I am not evil. Just because I do not want to hurt people. I do my best. It's just not bad enough."

Then Boris realised that something strange was happening in the castle: the dim daft dwarves had not returned to the shed and from the tower came the sound of screaming. Quietly he floated from the shed, and through a window of the tower.

At the far end of the vaulted hall the mini-skulls were enjoying target practice. They had mounted the dim daft dwarves on circles of wood which they spun round and round: as they did so other mini-skulls shot laser beams around the bodies. Julioso, Aliano and Benjio screamed and screamed.

Griselda was hanging upside down from the ceiling muttering fiercely, "Where is that useless skull? Never around when I want him. Totally useless."

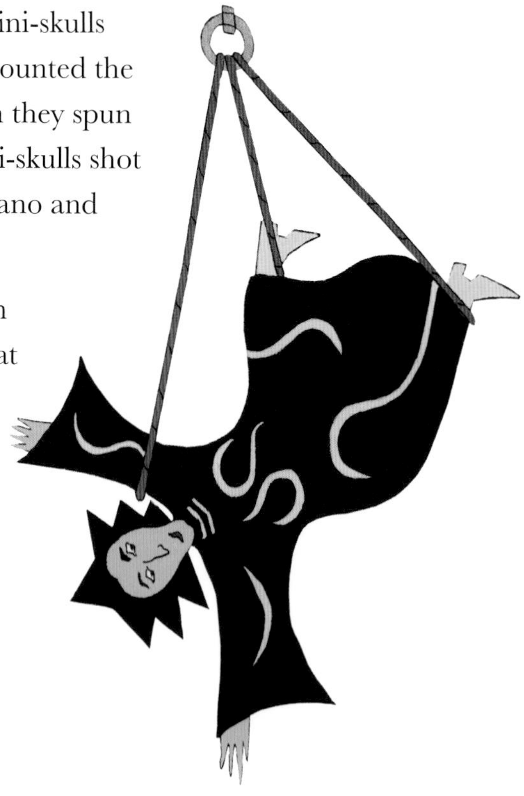

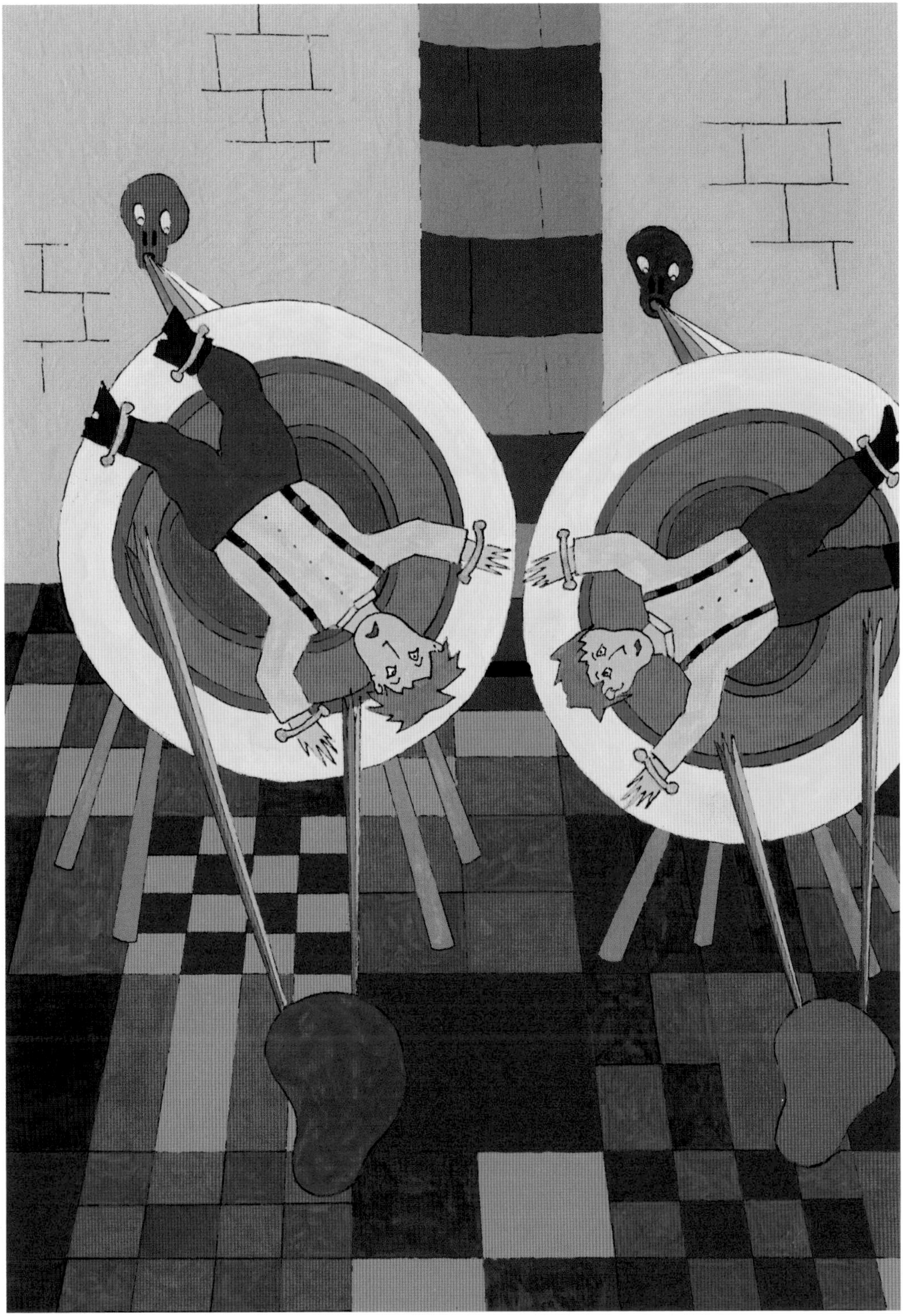

The mini-skulls were having fun before they ate the dwarves and witch, but even fun can be tiring. After spinning the dim daft dwarves round a thousand times Nip, Nit, Nik, Nix and Nib settled down in their box, sighed, "We'll eat them in the morning," and, tired out, fell asleep.

Boris floated to Griselda who greeted him with a hiss: "At last you pathetic lump of bone. Get me out of here."

Boris paused, and coming to a sudden resolution, said firmly, "Won't. You treat me so badly."

"You pathetic creep. Of course I treat you badly. When I send a thunderflash which echoes in your bony skull you adore it. It's your way of getting kicks."

"It is not!" cried Boris indignantly. "I would like you to treat me kindly. You got rid of me so that you could enjoy the company of five young skulls."

"Jealous! Jealous!" taunted Griselda.

"Perhaps I am, but I am not rescuing you unless you give me back my body."

"Your body! I don't have your body. Why on earth would I have your body? I bought you in the market."

"But you could help me get it back. Promise."

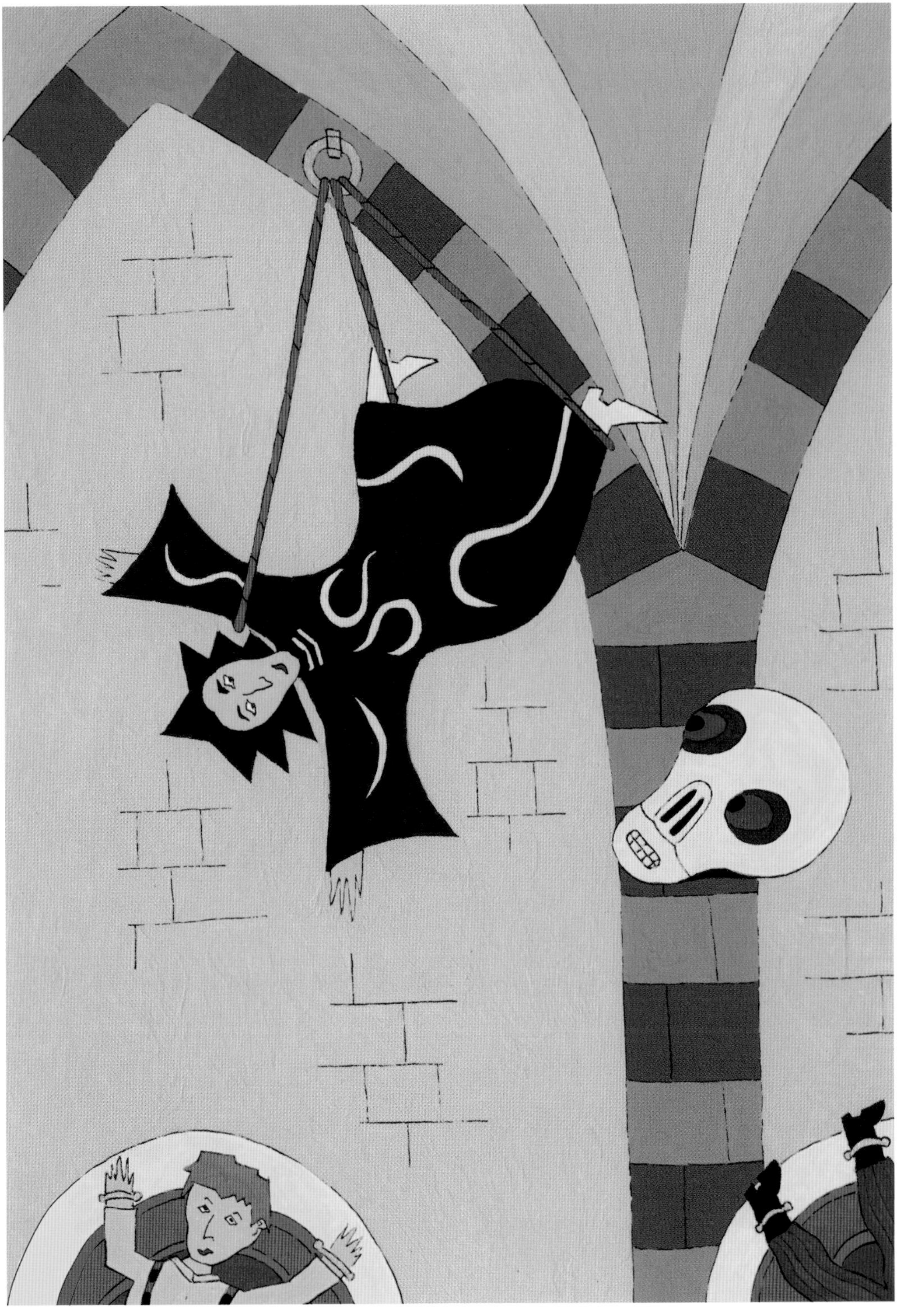

"Very well, I promise," muttered Griselda, keeping her fingers crossed behind her back so the promise did not count.

"Oh mistress! Thank you! Thank you!" stammered Boris (not noticing the fingers crossed behind her back). Quick as a flash he sent laser beams which cut through the ropes that tied Griselda to the ceiling. She landed on her head.

The five mini-skulls were awoken by the noise of Griselda's fall. Buzzing like fearsome flies, they rose out of their box, and headed straight for Boris, laser beams darting from their eye sockets, yelling "Burn! Burn! Burn! Burn him to bits!"

Boris was waiting for them. He did a somersault. Near the top of the vaulted ceiling laser beams shot out of his left eye socket, then his right, then repeat shots out of both eye sockets, in quick succession.

Griselda jumped up and down shouting, "Go Boris! Get them! Get them!" as Nip, Nit, Nik, Nix and Nib were blasted into tiny particles of dust. Even Griselda was impressed, murmuring to herself, "Boris is jealous of my toy boys. There must be evil in him after all. Perhaps all he needs is a little reconditioning – much cheaper than buying a new skull."

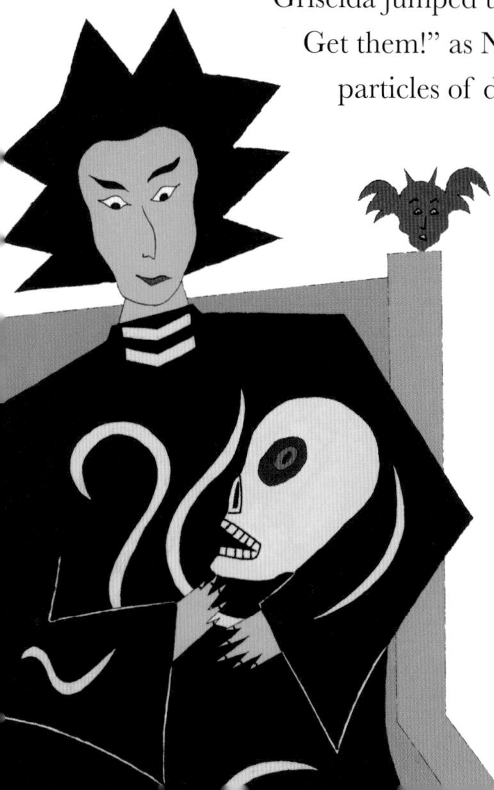

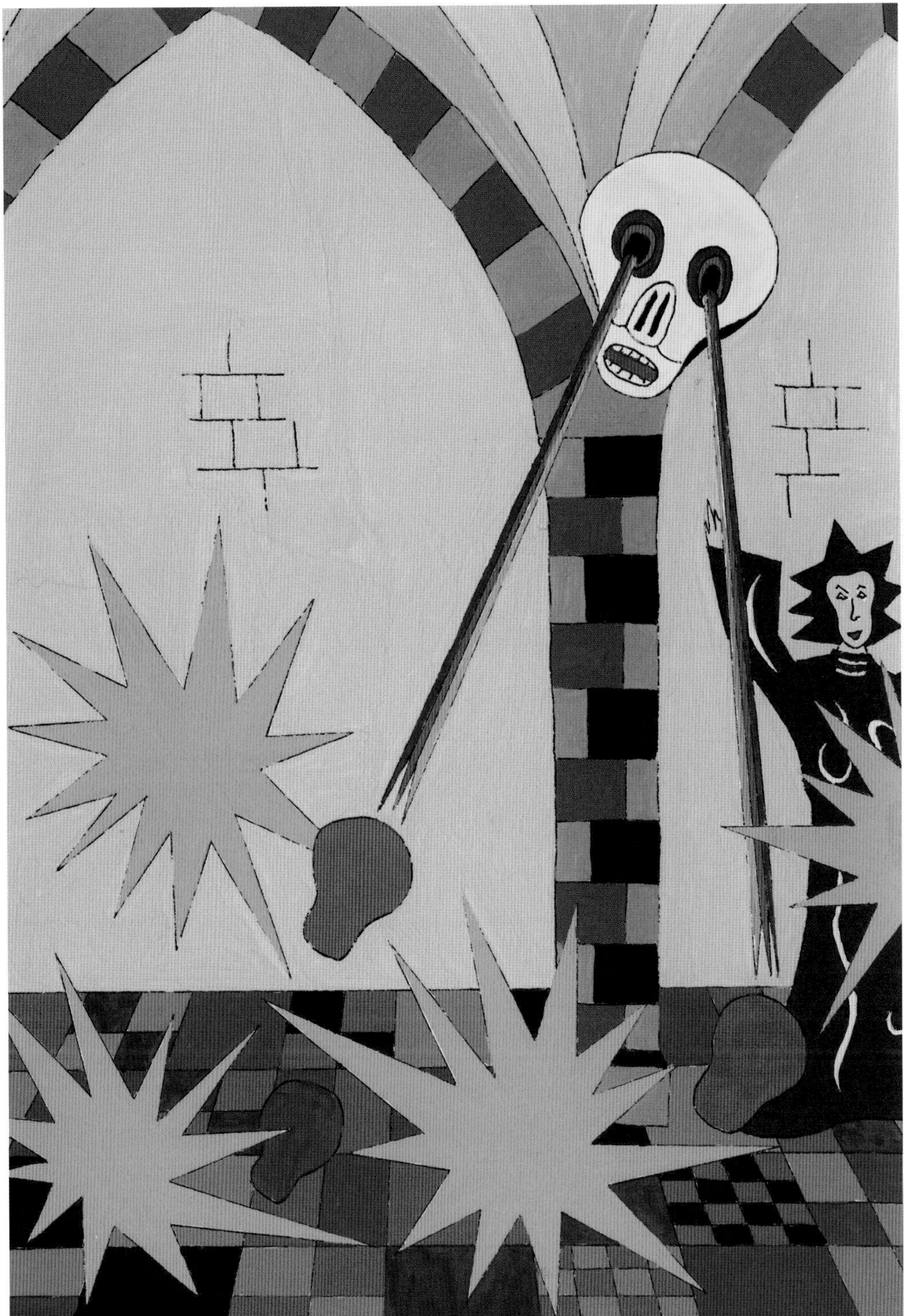

After Boris had blasted the mini-skulls he did a victory roll, triple somersaults and zoomed to Griselda, bubbling with excitement, "Did you see how I blasted the mini-skulls? I really got them."

"Boris, I did. You were not your normal useless self. Come to Griselda and I shall scratch your bony head."

"Mistress! That would be marvellous!"

Griselda sat down on her throne of slimy stone. Boris floated to her. She cradled him in her arms and scratched his bony head. The skull began to shake, his eye sockets to spin. "Oh mistress, this is fantastic!" Then swallowing hard, he asked, "Mistress, do you remember your promise?"

"What was that Boris?"

"About helping me get back my body."

"How did you lose it?"

Boris paused. "This morning I had a wonderful vision. I was a builder, young, strong and handsome."

"You must be joking!"

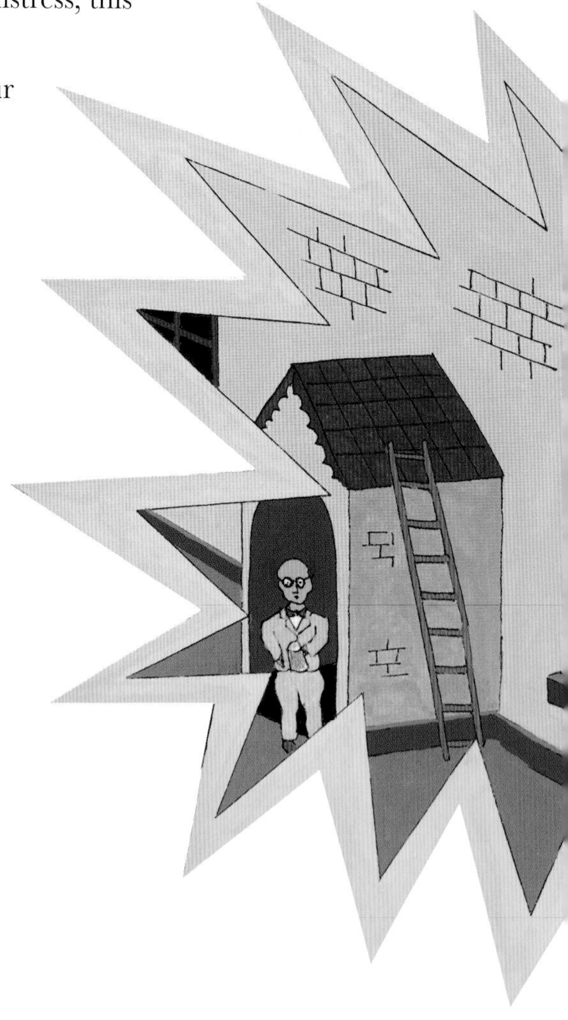

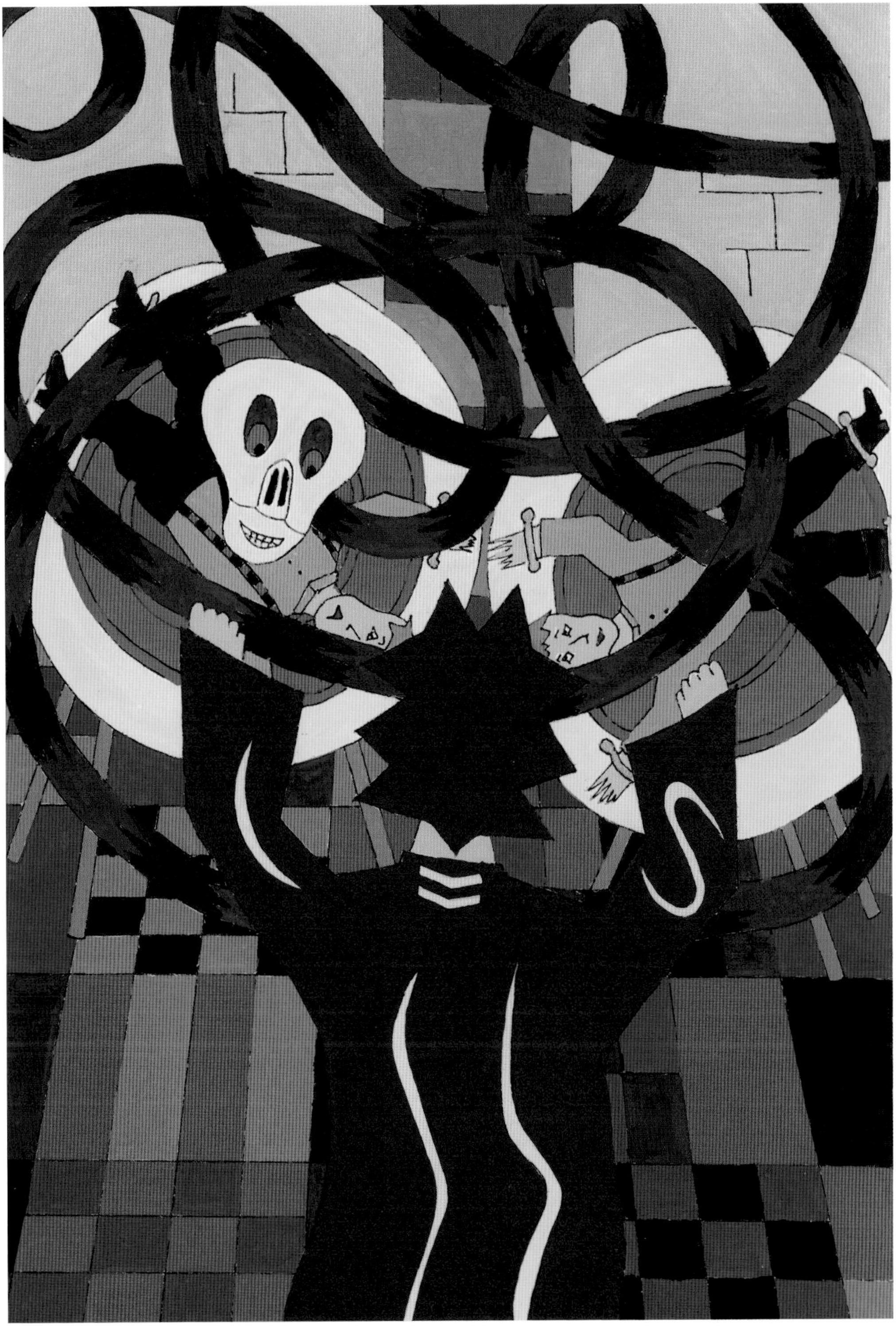

"All right. Once I was a builder. I remember going to Stench Manor to repair the roof. This fat man handed me a drink. Then he began to rub his hands in glee. I cannot remember anything after that."

"That was Charlie Stench!" cried Griselda. "He's a collector."

"What does he collect?"

"Bodies. He turns the heads into skulls, and sells some of them in the market. The drink would have sent you to sleep. Then Charlie would have popped you into his reconditioning machine, preserving your body for his collection and turning your head into a floating skull to sell in the market, where I bought it. He should have fitted out your skull with all the powers of evil, but in your case he failed."

"Mistress! Mistress! Mistress!" cried Boris bouncing up and down on her lap and getting thoroughly over-excited. "If he added my body to his collection, you could get it back."

"Perhaps," murmured Griselda thinking hard.

"Did I ever tell you that I was a great dancer?" asked Boris. "The Dashing White Sergeant. Strip the Willow. I did them all."

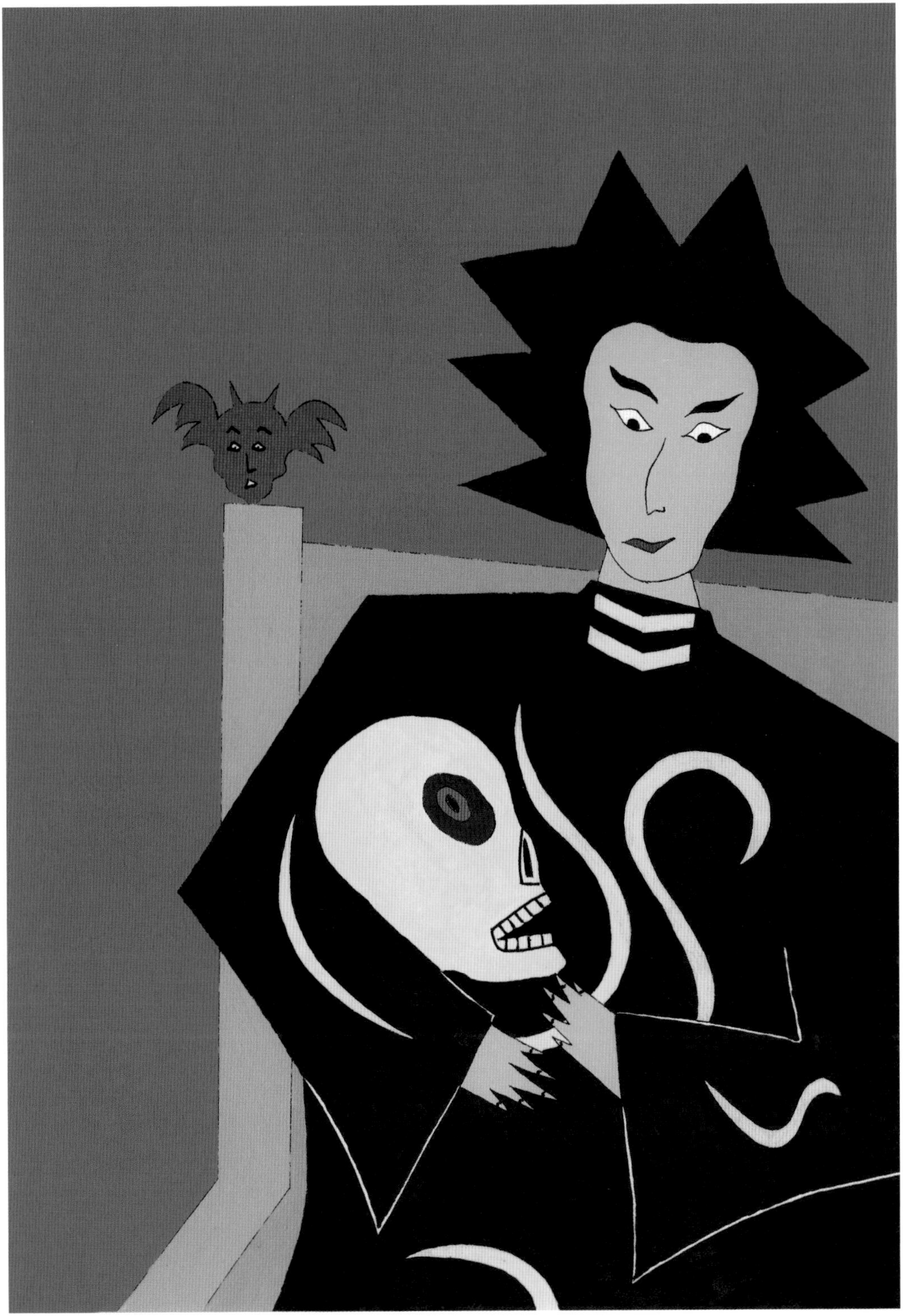

"Boris, I have no wish to know what you did with your body. But, very well. We shall go and find Charlie Stench. Stench Manor is on the far side of the forest. But first I must make a telephone call." Griselda went upstairs to her bedroom, lifted the phone and dialled. "Charlie, I want a word with you."

Charlie Stench lived in a rambling mansion with soaring turrets and towers. As a collector of bodies, he would preserve them from decay, but turn the heads into floating skulls with evil powers. Some of the skulls were still attached to their bodies, but others he sold in the market. The bodies he kept in catacombs beneath an ancient temple in the shape of a pyramid in the grounds of his mansion in the hills above Shoreham.

There were different corridors for different parts of his collection: the Men's Corridor, the Women's Corridor, the Children's Corridor (full of little children, some holding games), the Tourists' Corridor (a whole coachload of American tourists had driven into Stench Manor mistaking it for Knole House), the Sportsmen's Corridor (with specimens from every football team in the Premier League) and the Headless Corridor, in which stood the conditioning machine used to preserve the bodies and turn the heads into floating skulls. Charlie was a fat bulbous man with a shining bald head. He had popping eyes, glazed and dead except when he was talking about his collection when suddenly they began to shine and sparkle. He was very proud of his collection.

"Yes Griselda," he hissed.

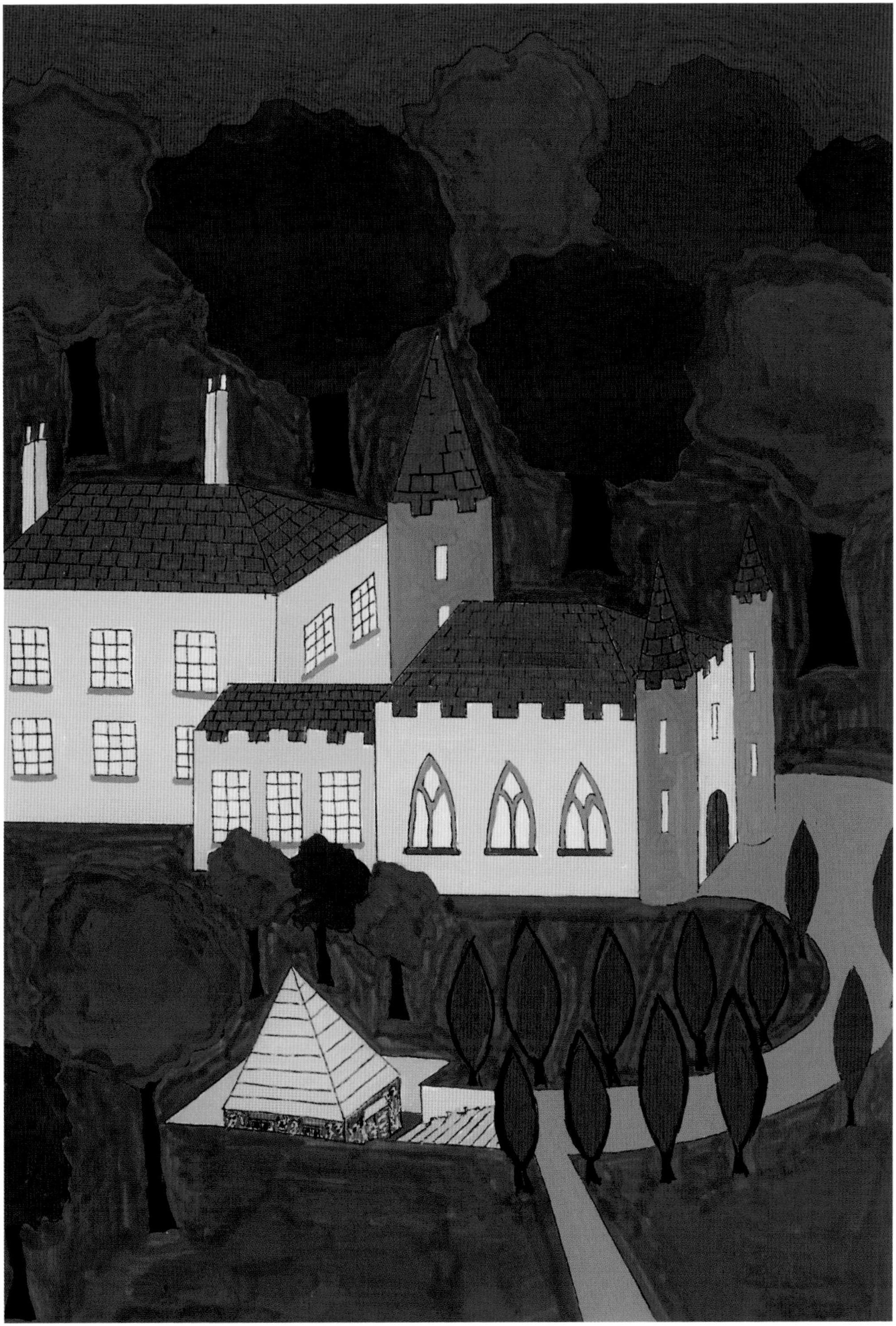

"Charlie, that skull I bought is totally useless. I tried to get him to blast some swordfish, but he wouldn't hurt them. Sometimes I think he is not evil at all."

"Must be part of the batch of 1982. I bombarded them with all the powers of evil, but somehow it did not work."

"But I want him really evil. I want him to fry people. I'll sue you on the guarantee for every cent you've got unless you recondition him free of charge."

"We do not live in the United States," protested Charlie haughtily.

"I'll sue you for every penny."

"All right," grumbled Charlie reluctantly.

"I'll bring him round tomorrow. And another thing. He's getting stupid thoughts about wanting to swim and dance and keeps going on about beautiful girls on the beaches of the south of France. When we come round you must make him think that his body is old and useless."

Well pleased, Griselda slammed down the receiver and murmured softly. "Excellent. A reconditioned Boris at no cost. I can't wait to see him fry people in the forest."

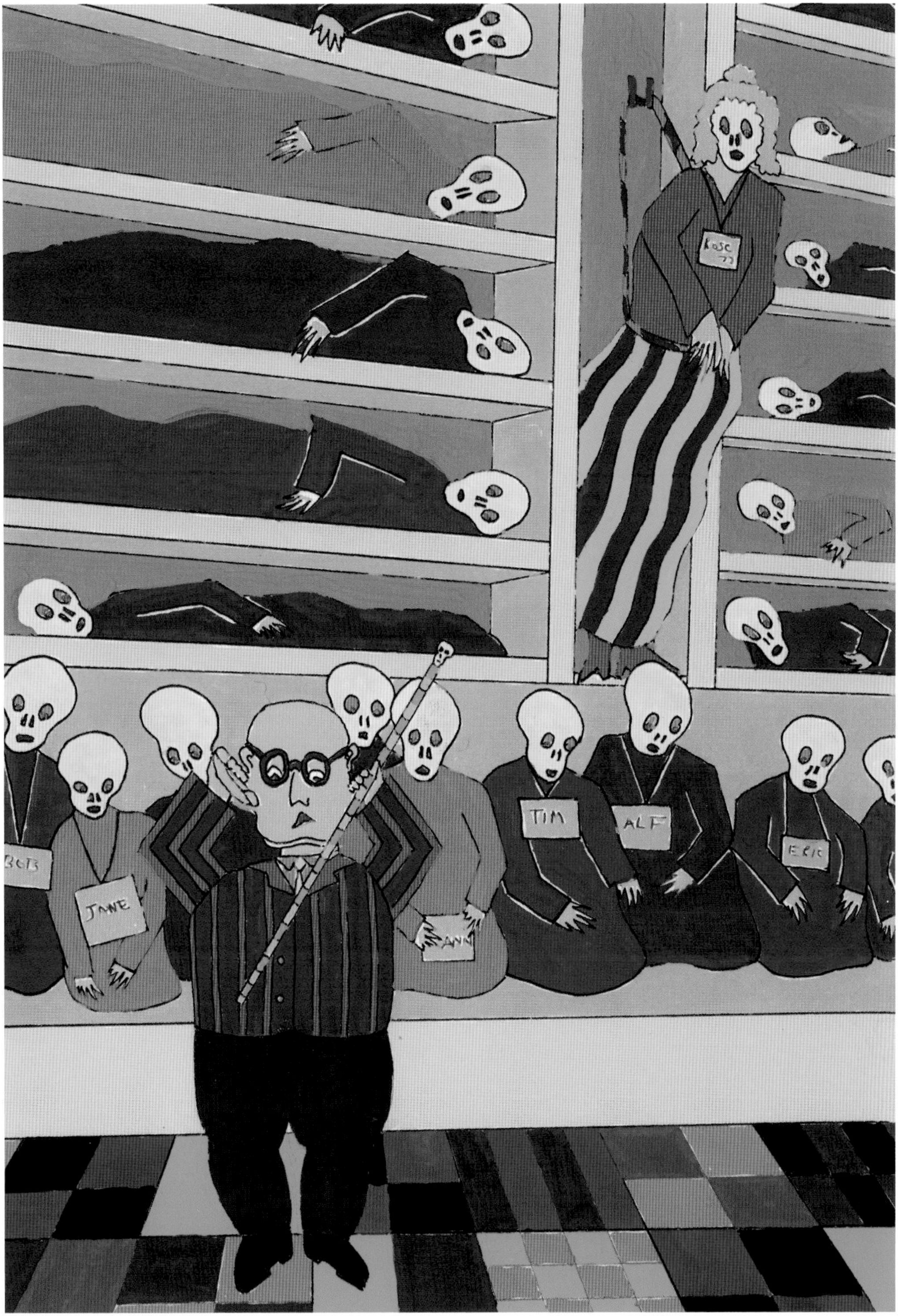
JANE
ANN
TIM
ALF
ERIC

When Griselda went upstairs to make the phone call in the privacy of her bedroom, Boris floated excitedly to the dim daft dwarves and freed them. They collapsed on the floor in a state of shock. "Julioso! Aliano! Benjio! I'm getting back my body! I'm getting back my body!" Boris cried.

"Oh great, Boris," muttered the exhausted dwarves without any enthusiasm, thinking a skull with a body would look pretty odd.

"When I get my body I'll teach you football, dancing, even punting."

"Great, Boris," muttered the dwarves: they had no idea what punting was, and thought it all sounded rather like hard work. Boris suddenly started whistling, and bouncing up and down, as if he were dancing a jig.

"Shut up, Boris!" screeched Griselda who had just reappeared looking strangely pleased with herself. "I have arranged for us to go and see Charlie Stench tomorrow evening. Until then, calm down. You know I can't stand whistling." So saying she raised her magic staff and sent a thunderflash which echoed in the bony skull.

"Oh mistress! There was no need for that. Even if I am a little over-excited."

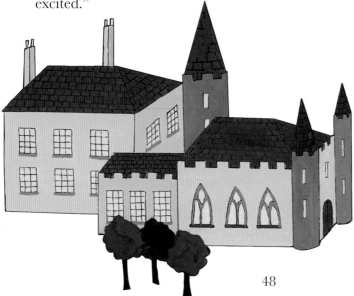

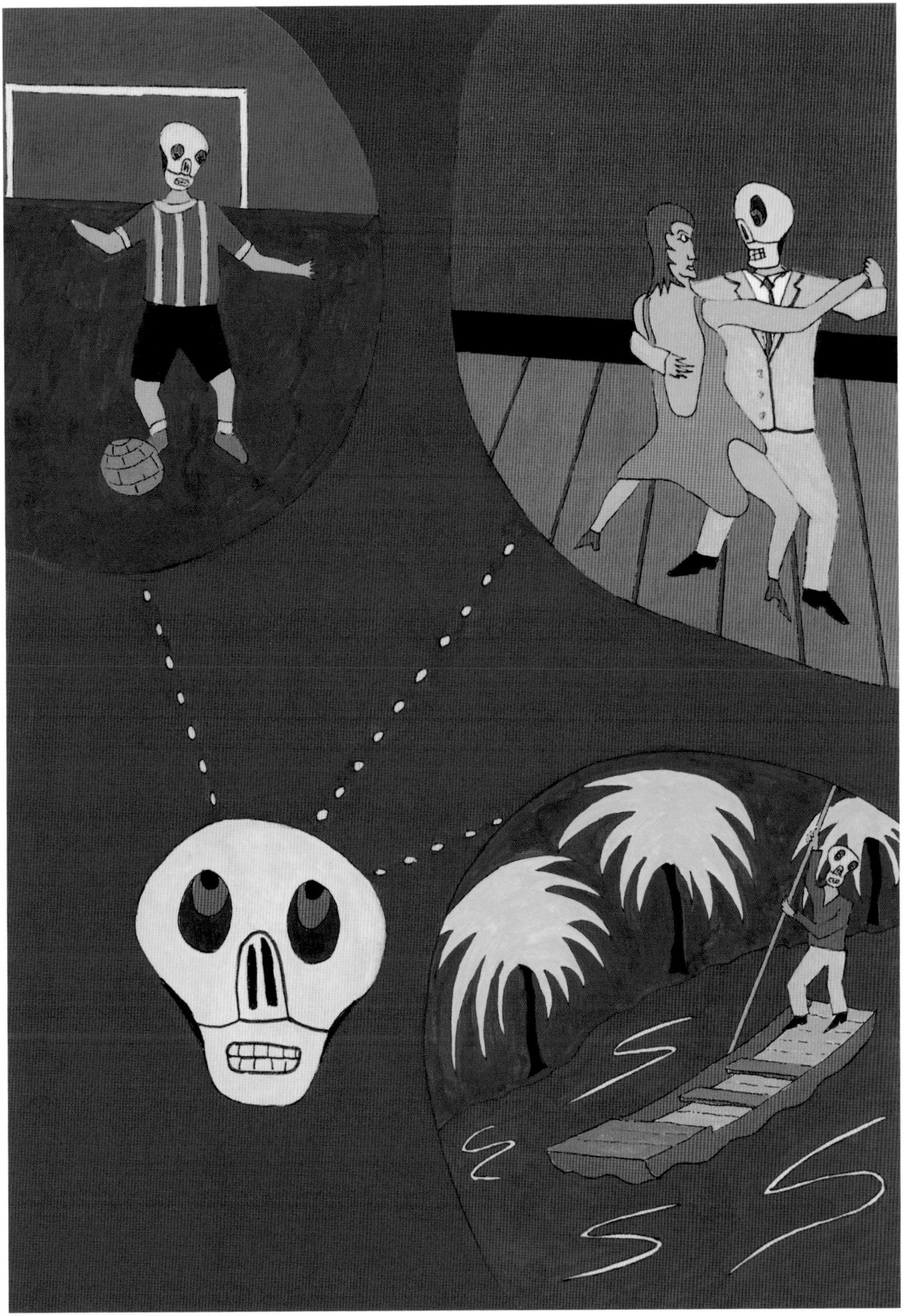

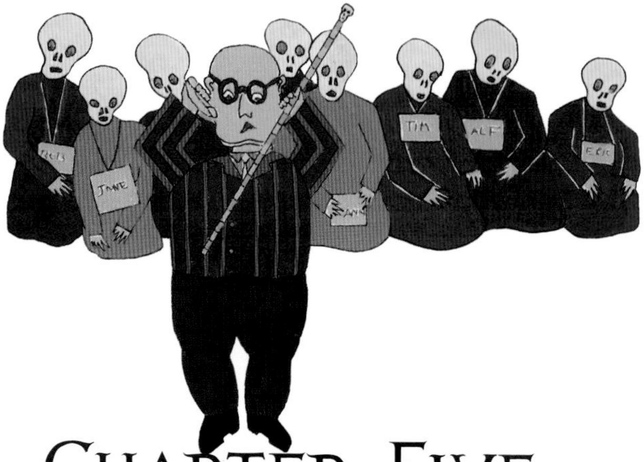
TIM
ALF

CHAPTER FIVE

Next day was an important day for the boys' parents. They were giving a lunch party. The boys' mother dressed the boys in their smartest clothes, and told them that they must be on their very best behaviour.

All went well until pudding. The boys' father was sitting at the table, with one High Court judge on one side, another High Court judge on the other. He was feeling pleased. Everything was going well. The party would help his career. Or so he thought.

At that moment Benjamin entered the room. He was carrying a supersoaker 500 – a high velocity pump-action water-pistol. With a cry of "I hate Dad!" he raised the water pistol and proceeded to soak his father, missing the High Court judges, and all the other guests, who murmured to each other, "Damn good shot!"

The reaction of Benjamin's father was less positive. Struggling to his feet, water dripping down his face, he tried to appear in total command of the situation – then completely lost his cool and screamed, "You little brat!"

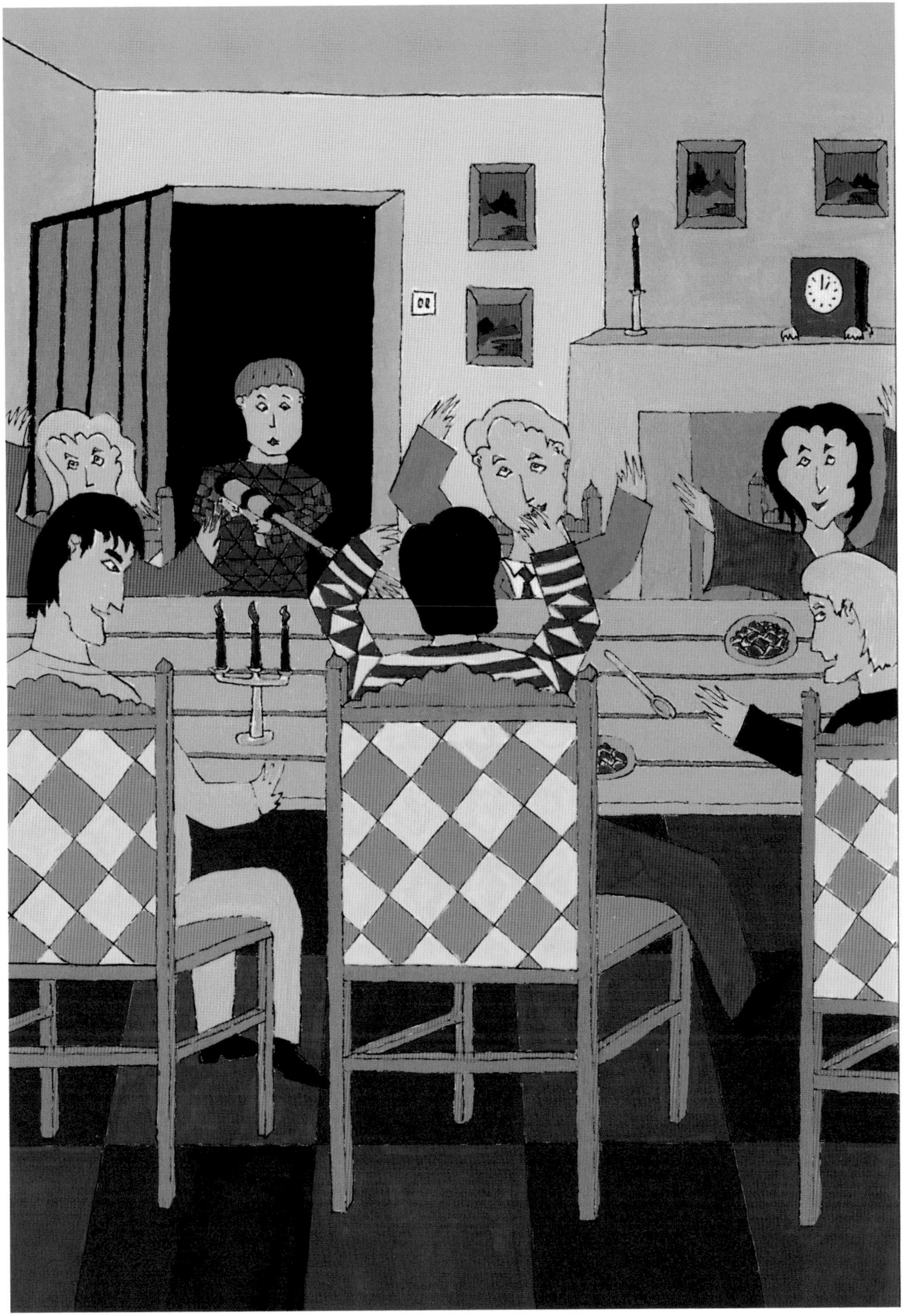

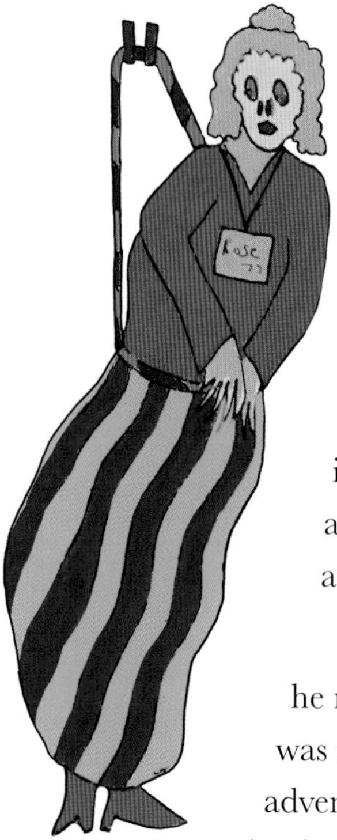

Benjamin ran, his father in pursuit, shouting loudly, shaking his fist. Benjamin darted through the sitting room, out into the garden. As his father grabbed the supersoaker, Benjamin picked up the garden hose, and turning it on, soaked his father from head to foot. From that time on whenever Benjamin's father met a colleague with a young daughter he would be introduced as "Benjamin's father" and the girl would go all gooey-eyed at the thought of the little hero (or monster as his father thought of him).

Later that afternoon as Benjamin sat in his bedroom, he realised that this time he had gone too far. There was nothing for it but to run away. He would become an adventurer, sail the seven seas, climb mountains, explore the Arctic wastes. That would make his parents sorry. Silently he pushed back the bedroom shutter, climbed out the window and carefully slid down the tiled roof above the ancient bread oven until he reached the ground. Creeping through the garden gate he ran up the road towards the station, across the main road, then up the hill into the woods.

At the top of White Hill Benjamin left the path. Soon he was completely lost. The skies darkened: it was going to rain. He struggled through a thick hedge and found himself in a garden. He looked for shelter. Not far from the mansion was a pyramid held up by huge statues, the door a web of tangled arms. Benjamin crept inside. The door slammed shut. Creeping down the stairs he realised in horror that along the walls were the bodies of the dead. Benjamin was trapped.

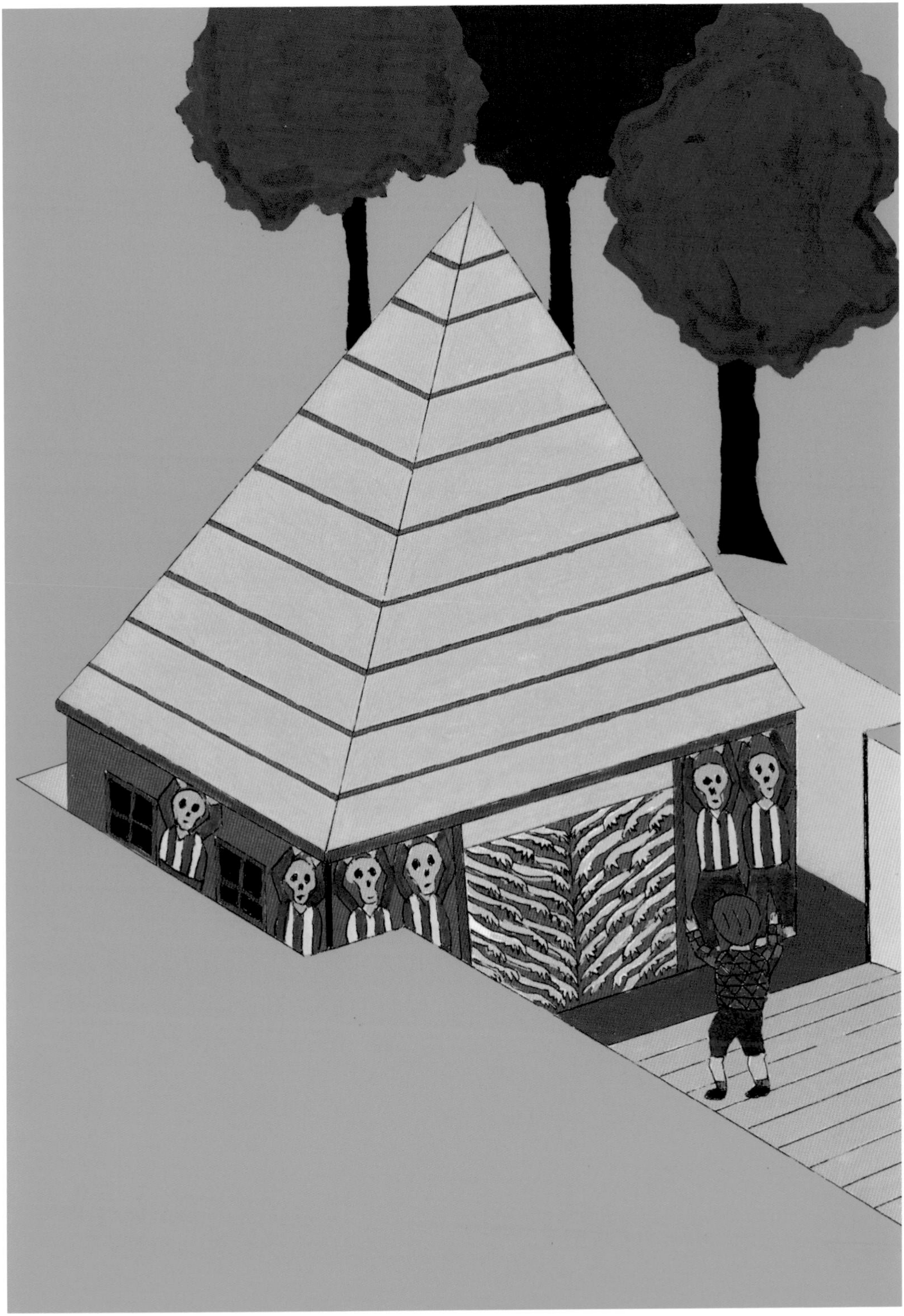

Snuggle ran to Julius and Alexander, and cried, "Benje has run away. He is in great danger. Griselda is about to recondition Boris, to make him completely evil. We must hurry."

"Snuggle! What's that?" Julius asked pointing to a little bag around the cat's neck.

"Something from the Gardener. Open it and see".

Julius bent down, pulled open the bag, and a small plant jumped out and gave a bow.

"Boys, may I introduce Tilney, the most precious of plants."

"Hi Tilney!" cried the boys.

"Miss Tilney to you!" replied the plant primly.

"We do beg your pardon, Miss Tilney. Are you a precious plant? Do you have the power to reverse evil magic?"

"But of course," said Snuggle. "That's what precious plants do. Now, Tilney, get back in the bag. We must hurry."

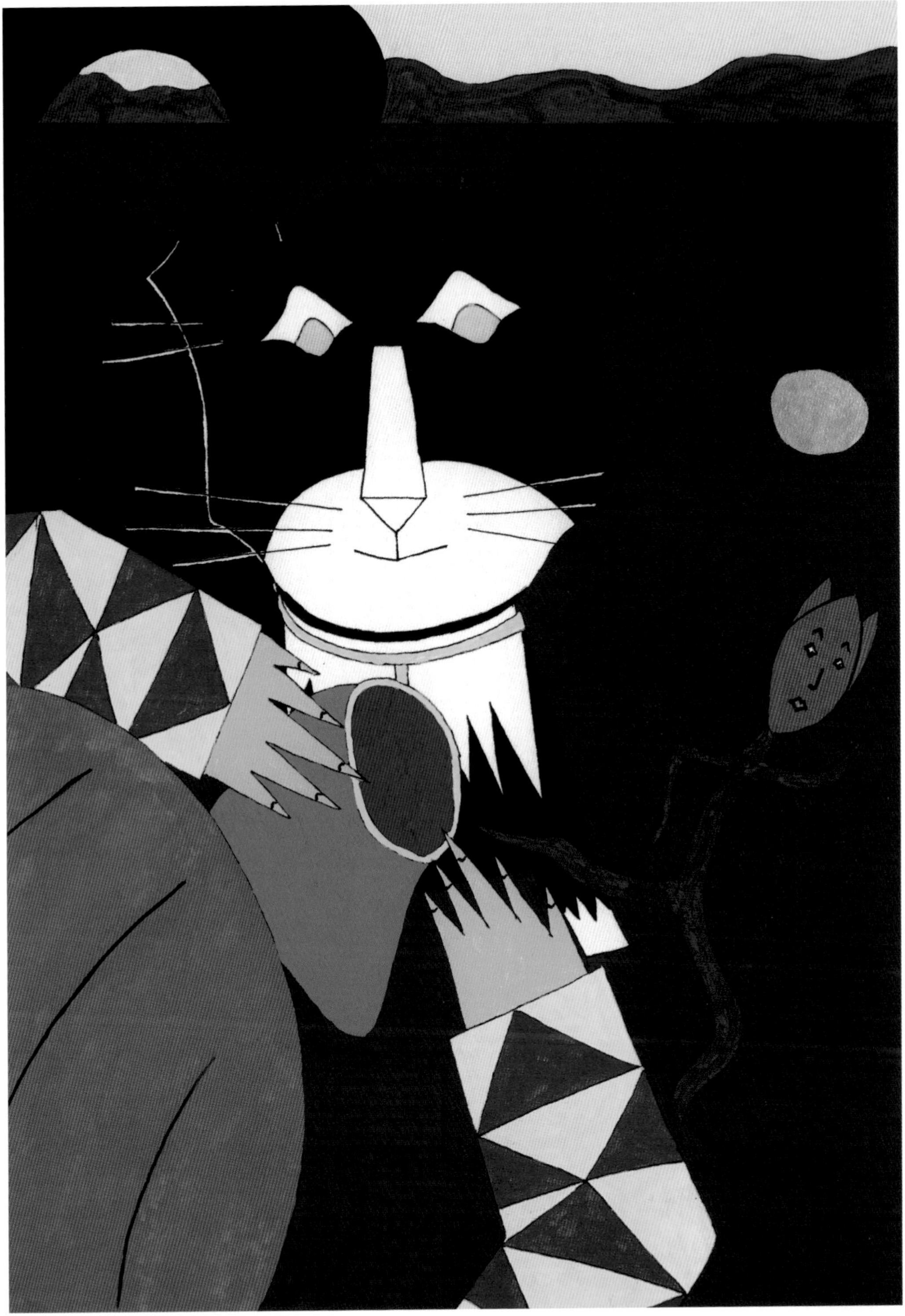

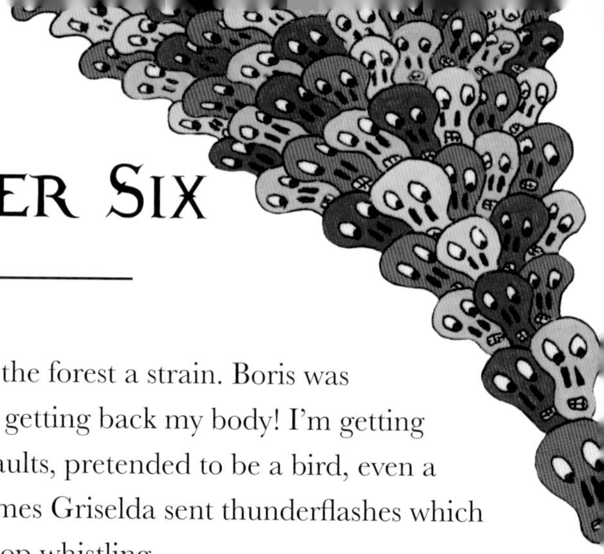

Chapter Six

Griselda found the walk through the forest a strain. Boris was completely hyper. Hissing "I'm getting back my body! I'm getting back my body!" he did triple somersaults, pretended to be a bird, even a fighter pilot. No matter how many times Griselda sent thunderflashes which echoed in his skull, Boris could not stop whistling.

"Boris, shut up!" howled Griselda. "The noise is ghastly." The forest got darker and darker, more and more creepy, until at the far side they reached a high thorn hedge surrounding Stench Manor. Griselda raised her magic staff: she and Boris passed through the hedge.

Stench Manor lay before them, soaring towers and turrets and in the middle of the grounds the small temple. Griselda went straight to the temple, pushed open the great doors in the shape of twisted arms and hurried down the stone steps to a vault of yellow stone. Along both sides of the corridors were bodies lined up in racks with neat labels round the neck or wrists, identifying name and index number. On the shelves above the racks stood the prize specimens in the Stench collection: whole families, mums, dads and children, some holding toys. At the far end of the main corridor stood a plump, bulbous man with bulging eyes, holding a book, shaking his head and muttering to himself, "Batch of '82. Conditioning went wrong. Did not turn out evil at all."

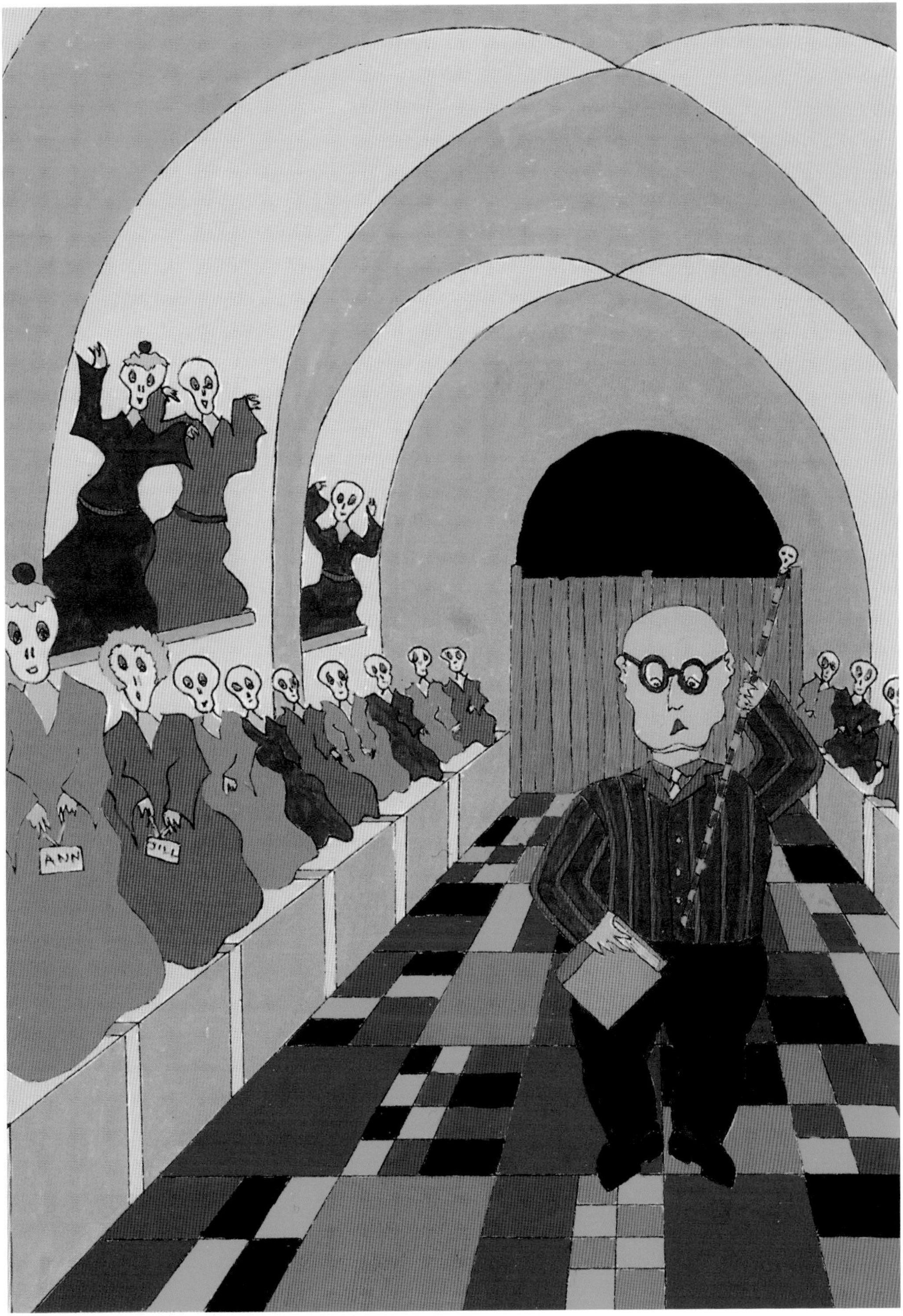
ANN
JILL

"Oh no! Not Griselda!" murmured Benjamin as he ran silently down the corridors, squeezed in between two headless bodies and pretended to be dead.

Griselda strode forward, calling out a cheerful greeting, "Good to see you Charlie. This is Boris. I think you have met before."

"Part of the batch of '82. I am sorry, Griselda. A bad mistake. Did not do my reputation any good at all."

"Boris is looking for his body. Show it to him."

"But of course." Charlie rubbed his hands in glee, his dull dead eyes began to sparkle, his fat body to glow with pride. "All bodies are labelled and indexed. I just have to look Boris up in the index." Charlie moved to a wooden cabinet, and pulled out a file. "Ah yes. Boris Austin. Male. Then dates of birth and capture. Just follow me to the Headless Corridor."

Boris was jigging up and down looking for his body. He looked at the middle of the headless corridor (big, fit men in the prime of life) but no label had his name. "No! No!" cried Charlie. "Look at the end." Swiftly Boris floated along the row. The bodies got older and older, more and more decrepit. Near the end of the row was a bent, shrivelled body of an aged man. Boris's jaw dropped as he read the label, "Boris Austin". (He did not know that the labels had been swapped by Charlie after receiving Griselda's telephone call.)

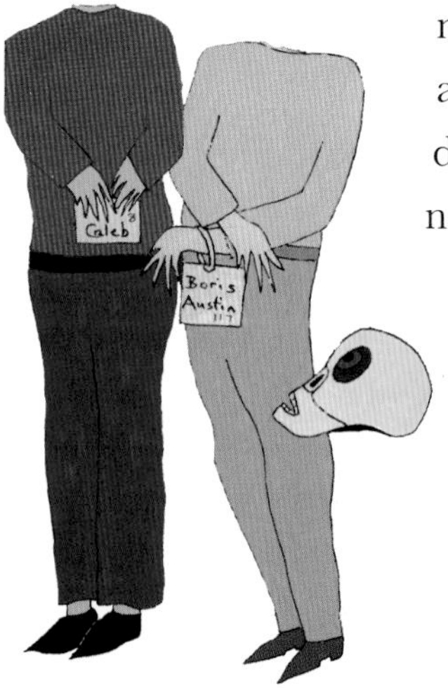
Caleb
Boris Austin

"Oh!" cried Boris in shock. "I didn't know that I was as old as that. I had a vision of myself. I was a builder, who came to fix the roof, not an old man about to drop dead."

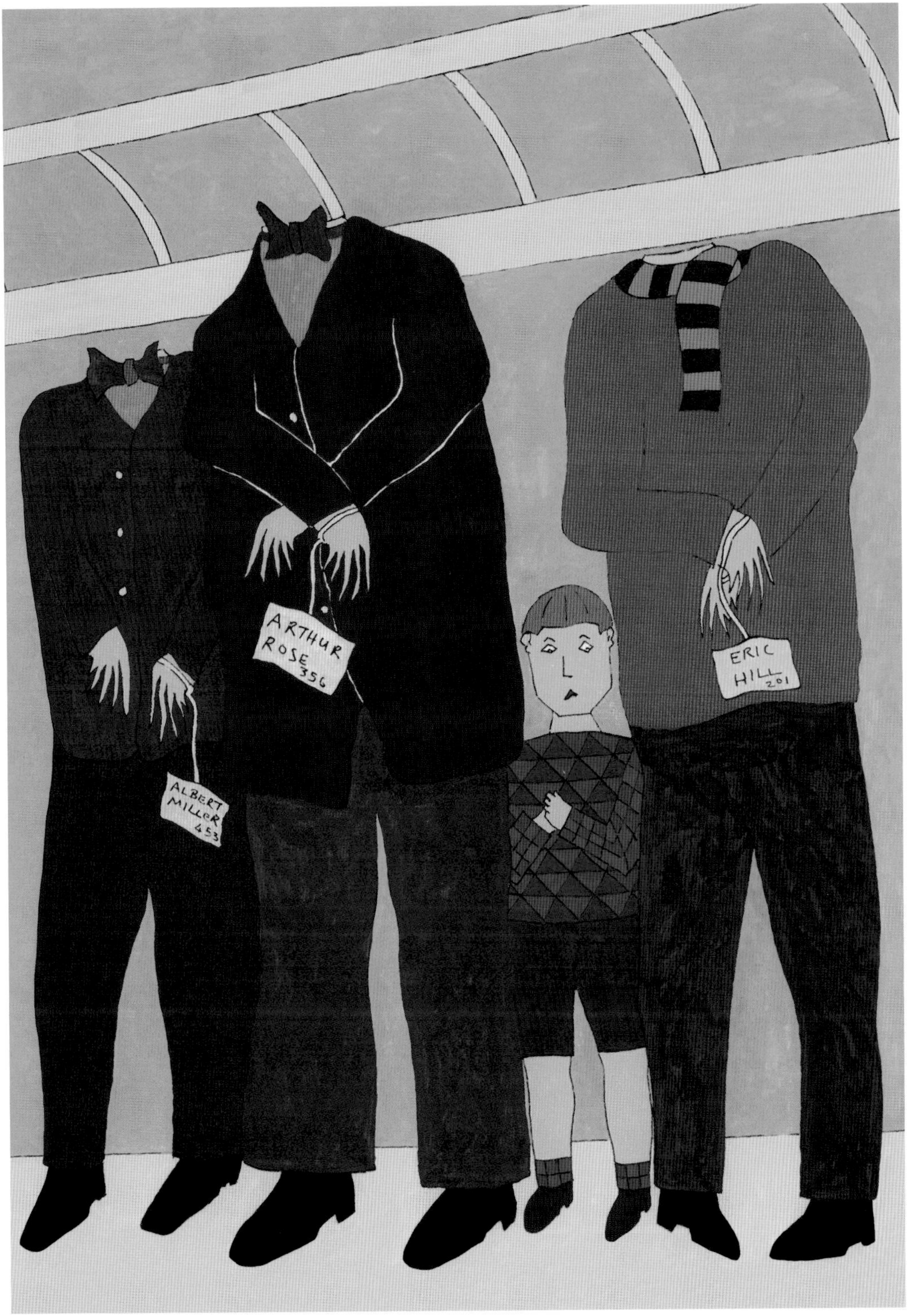
ALBERT MILLER 453
ARTHUR ROSE 356
ERIC HILL 201

Charlie shook his head. "The conditioning of a skull plays strange tricks on the mind. No doubt you thought that you were young, handsome, good at dancing. Pure fantasy. As you can see you were an old man, completely past it, almost dead. I did you a favour in making you into a skull. You would have been dead within the week."

Griselda rubbed her hands in triumph. "Boris you are an idiot. No one would want a body like that. Girls in the south of France would not think much of it."

Sorrowfully Boris shook his head, blinking away a tear. "All my dreams! I was a fool. If I got back that body I would be dead within a week. I had better stay a skull."

"A wise decision," hissed Griselda gleefully. "But there is one thing I must attend to whilst I am here." She took a piece of paper out of her pocket, handed it to Charlie, and murmured fiercely, "He is still under guarantee."

"Yes, yes, of course. Something went wrong with the conditioning. I shall fix it." Charlie turned to Boris. "Mr Austin, I am glad that your body can stay in my collection: although old and pathetic, my collection would not be complete without it. But if you would come through here, there is something I would like to show you."

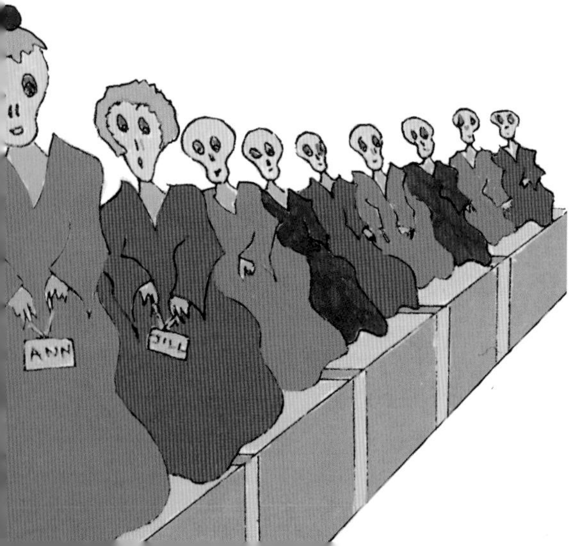
ANN
JILL

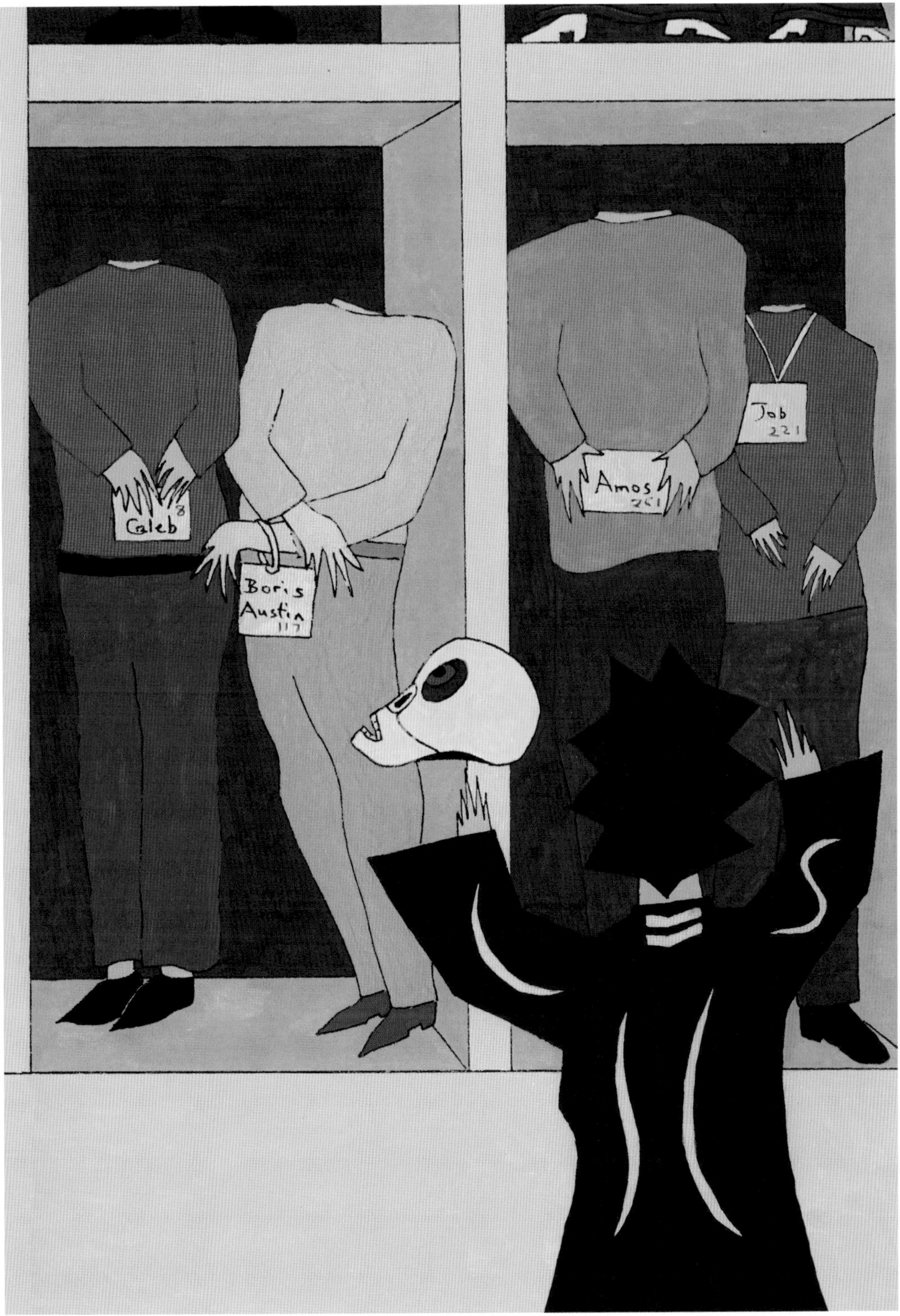
Caleb 8
Boris Austin 117
Amos 261
Job 221

Trustingly, Boris floated after Charlie Stench who opened the door of the conditioning machine. "After you, Mr Austin. After you." Boris found himself in a small windowless room lined with lead and, as Charlie slammed the door behind him, cried out in alarm, "Fooled again! Oh why am I so trusting?"

"How long will the reconditioning take?" asked Griselda.

"Not long," replied Charlie. "I just have to press this switch."

"You're sure that this time he will become evil through and through?" queried Griselda.

"But of course. Conditioning cannot fail twice."

"That is good," sighed Griselda, rubbing her hands in glee. "At last I shall have a skull to float through the forest and fry people. But before you press the switch, I would like to see Boris's body." (It was many years since last she saw it).

Charlie's eyes sparkled with pride. "Oh, it is one of the best in my collection." He took Griselda past the end of the row where in a recess he had hidden a young man of medium height, just over thirty, in the very prime of life.

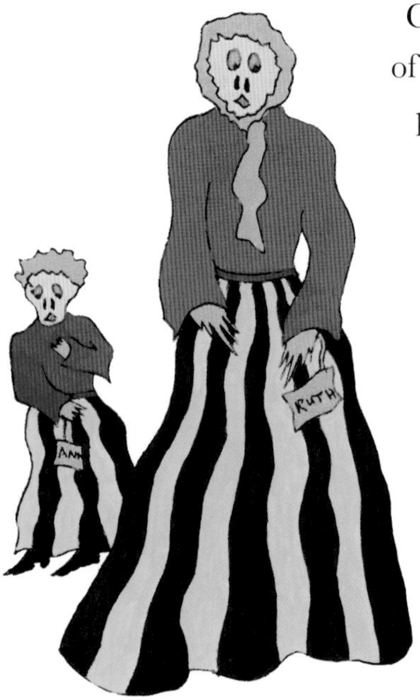
RUTH

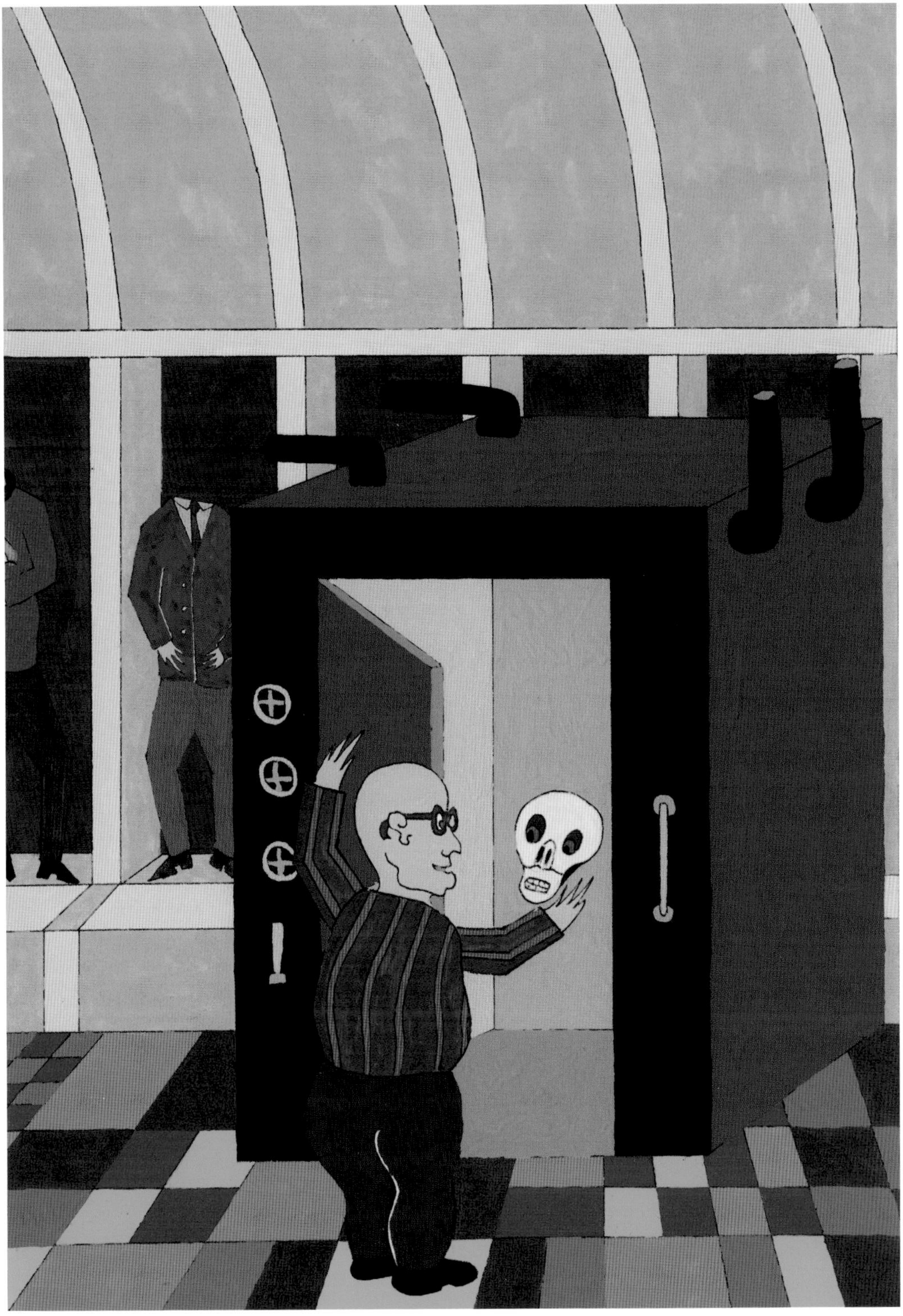

"Hmmm. Not bad … not bad at all," Griselda purred, looking carefully at the body. "Whatever am I saying!" Hastily she corrected herself. "Not bad as bodies go. But I have no interest in such things. I only want a skull. You had better press the switch."

As Charlie stretched out to press the switch his eyes wandered to the other side of the corridor. He froze in alarm. There was a body with a head. Leaning towards Griselda he whispered in her ear, "There is a stranger in the collection. Look at that small body trying to keep still."

"Benjamin," murmured Griselda, licking her lips, "I have always wanted to eat him."

"Well, you cannot have him. I saw him first. I shall add him to my collection." So saying, Charlie raised a hand and clicked his fingers. Silently, skulls rose from bodies in the Men's Corridor and floated to their master. "Get that boy," Charlie commanded. "But do not damage him. I want him for my collection."

In horror Benjamin opened his eyes, jumped out from the gap between the headless bodies, and began to run, a swarm of skulls hurrying after him, buzzing like angry wasps. He reached the bottom of the stairs. He had begun to climb when the skulls got him. Sinking their teeth into his shirt and trousers they lifted him, screaming, high into the air, then dropped him gently between the Body Collector and the conditioning machine.

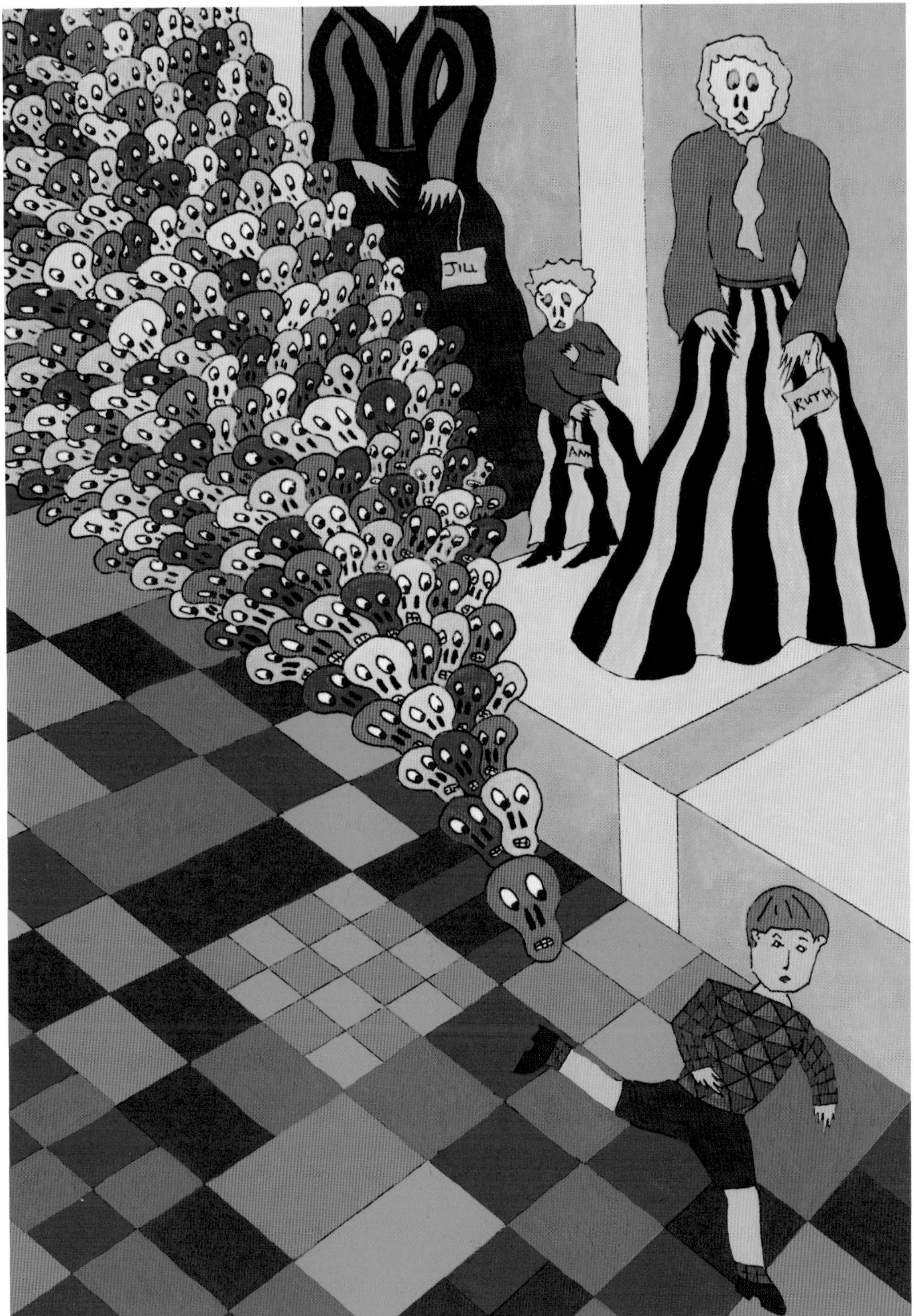
JILL
RUTH

CHAPTER SEVEN

At that moment Snuggle, Julius and Alexander entered the temple. Silently they crept down the stairs, as Charlie and Griselda quarrelled over Benjamin.

"You've got lots of boys in your collection. I've always wanted Benjamin on toast. Let me eat him."

"I saw him first. He's got a nice little body. Just right for my collection."

Snuggle and the boys reached the bottom of the stairs. "What do you want us to do?" whispered the boys.

"I need a diversion. Distract their attention. Do not worry about the skulls when they come to get you. Charlie does not like damaged bodies in his collection."

Julius turned to Alexander. "You go that way. I'll go this. When I raise my arm, start to run and scream." So saying, Julius walked quietly towards the Tourist's Corridor, Alexander towards the Sportsmen's Corridor. Alexander was looking at the Premier League footballers, and laughing silently at the Tottenham Hotspur player (his dad supported Spurs, he and Benjamin their rivals Arsenal) when Julius raised his arm. Both began to run and scream.

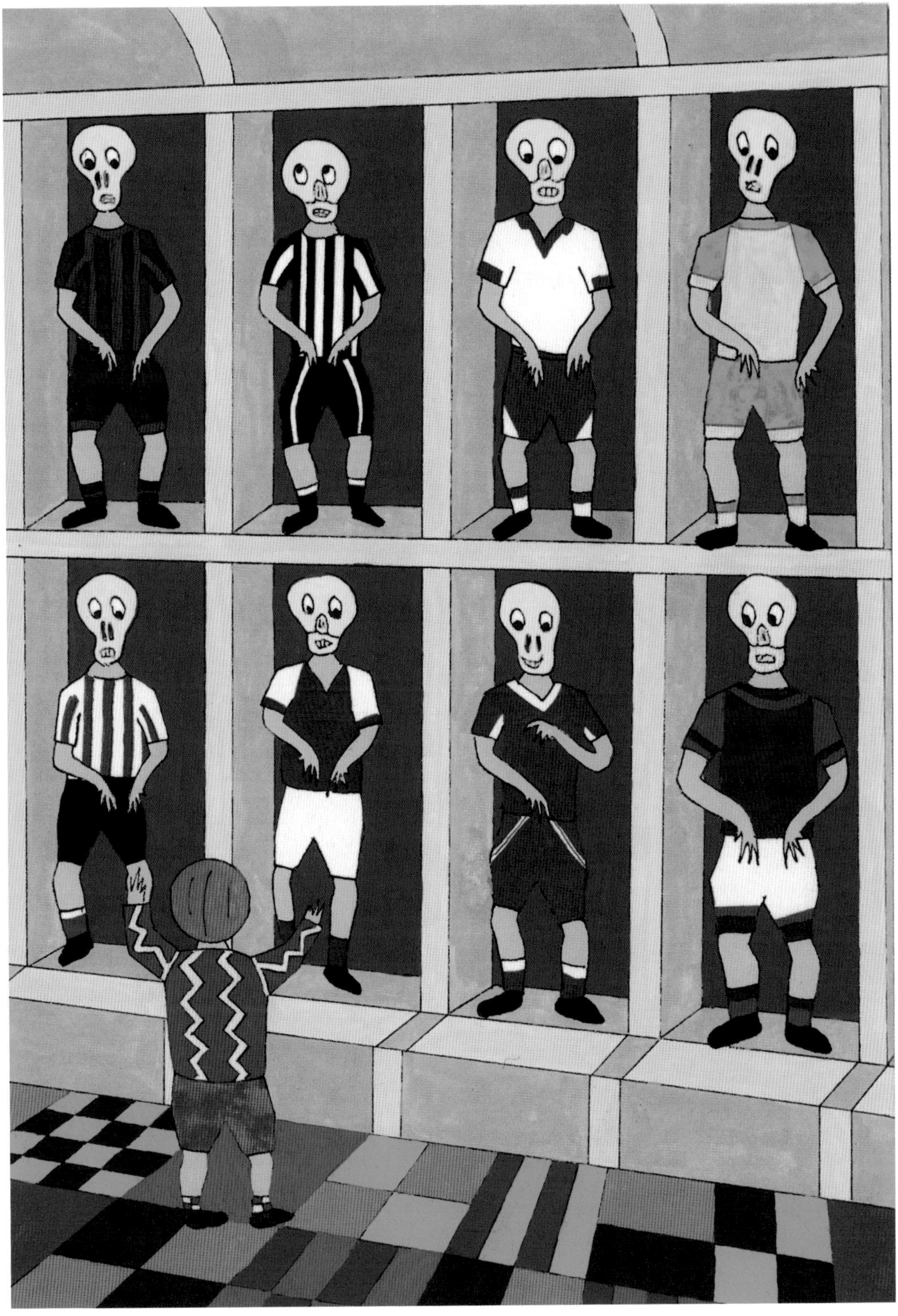

Charlie and Griselda stopped quarrelling. "Oh roast Julius! Stewed Alexander! How absolutely scrumptious!" enthused Griselda.

"More bodies for my collection," cried Charlie as he raised his arm and clicked his fingers. "Get them, skulls." The skulls divided into two swarms and set off at Charlie's direction.

Alexander had just reached the Chelsea player (smirk on his skull, as self-satisfied in death as he had been in life) when one swarm grabbed and lifted him, kicking and screaming, and dropped him at the feet of the Body Collector.

The other swarm reached Julius just as he was passing a particularly fat tourist with camera round his neck, baseball cap perched on his glowing skull, cigar between perfect teeth, chomping his approval, as Julius was lifted kicking and screaming into the air. The skulls laid him gently on top of Alexander.

As the skulls carried Julius and Alexander to them, Charlie and Griselda did not see Snuggle moving in the shadows, creeping round behind them. Silently Snuggle turned into a warrior, half man, half cat, took the bag from his neck, lifted Tilney out of the bag, and raised his arm to open the door of the conditioning machine. Then Griselda saw him. "Snuggle!" she screamed. "And what is that at his feet?"

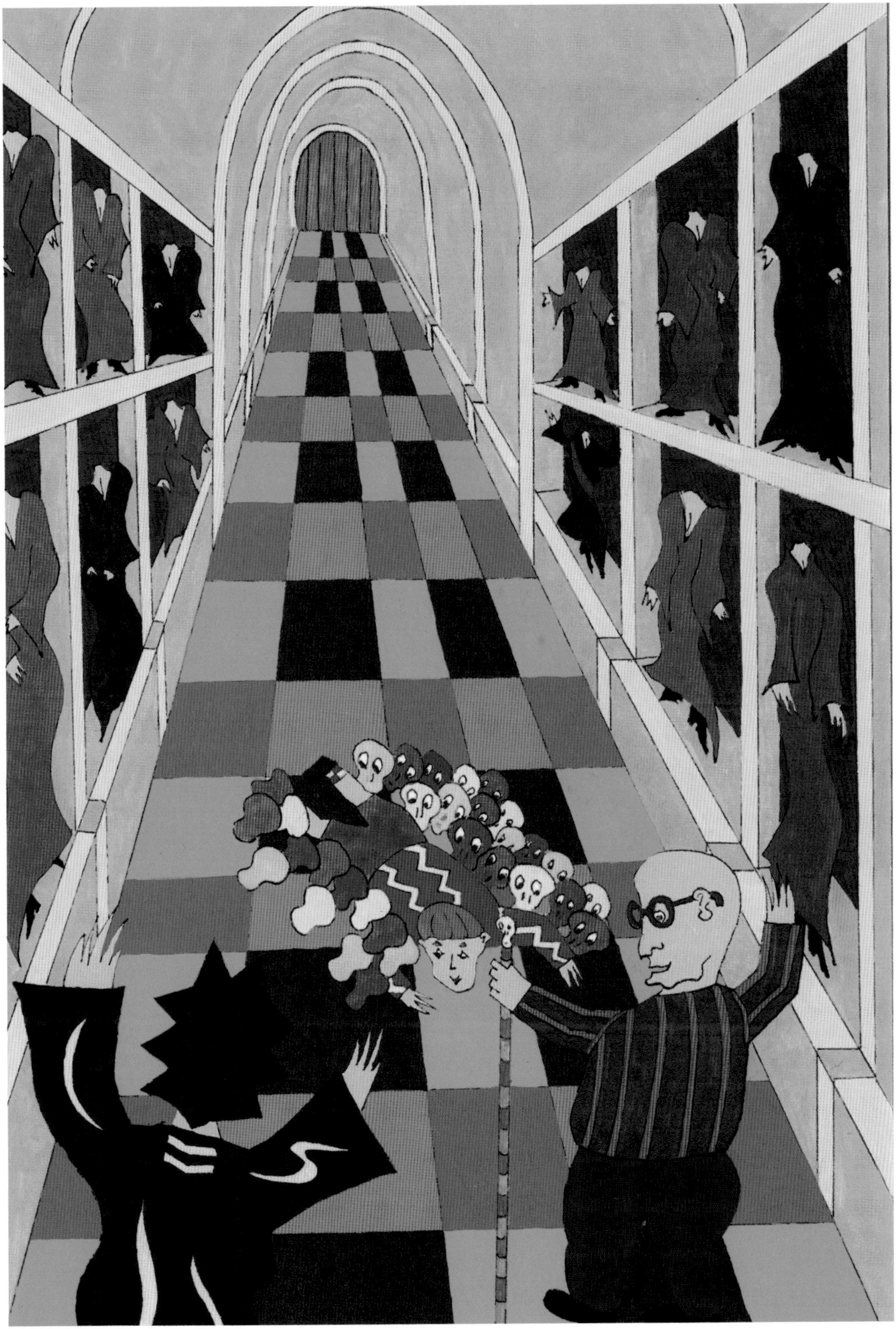

"A precious plant!" gasped Charlie in a panic realising what Snuggle was about to do. "He's going to reverse the magic! He's going to destroy my collection! Kill that cat!" Charlie and Griselda raised their arms in unison. Evil rays crackled from their finger tips. Snuggle raised his shield, and as the rays bounced around him shouted, "To me, Benje. Behind my back." At Snuggle's command Benjamin rolled away from Charlie and Griselda, and scurried behind the cat. "Now open that door." As rays of evil magic flashed and crashed around about them, Benjamin pulled the door ajar. Tilney jumped in. Pushing Benjamin to the ground and shielding him with his body, Snuggle kicked the door shut and pressed the switch.

As the door slammed shut a second time Boris groaned again, "Oh why am I so trusting?" Then as Snuggle pressed the switch, from every side of the lead cell Boris was bombarded by the powers of evil, with terrible images of war and famine, of pain and cruelty. But with Tilney by his side the results were surprising. No matter how terrible the image, somewhere Boris always found a precious plant. Tilney whispered quietly to him, "Look at the precious plant: block out the evil." Heavy guns thundered. Men clambered out of trenches thick in mud. Machine guns rattled. Bodies fell. But all Boris saw was a tiny precious plant of purest orange and green. Then another. And another. Until suddenly in an explosion of orange and green, all around him were flowers, and he found himself in a garden where plants grew wild and free. The Gardener raised his arms in friendly greeting. Triumphant but exhausted, Boris blacked out.

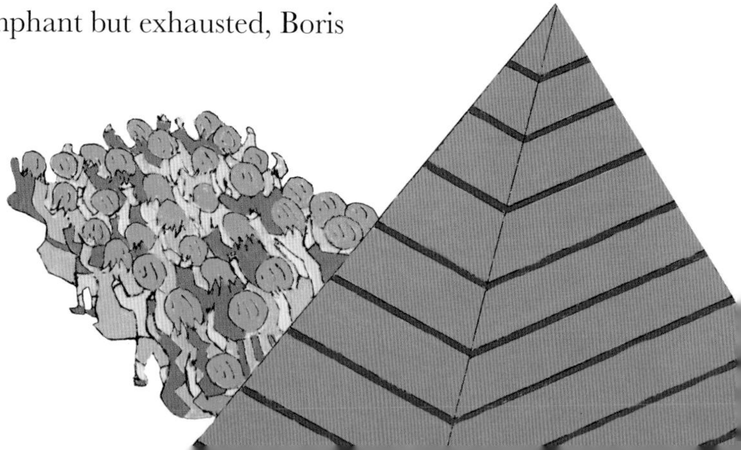

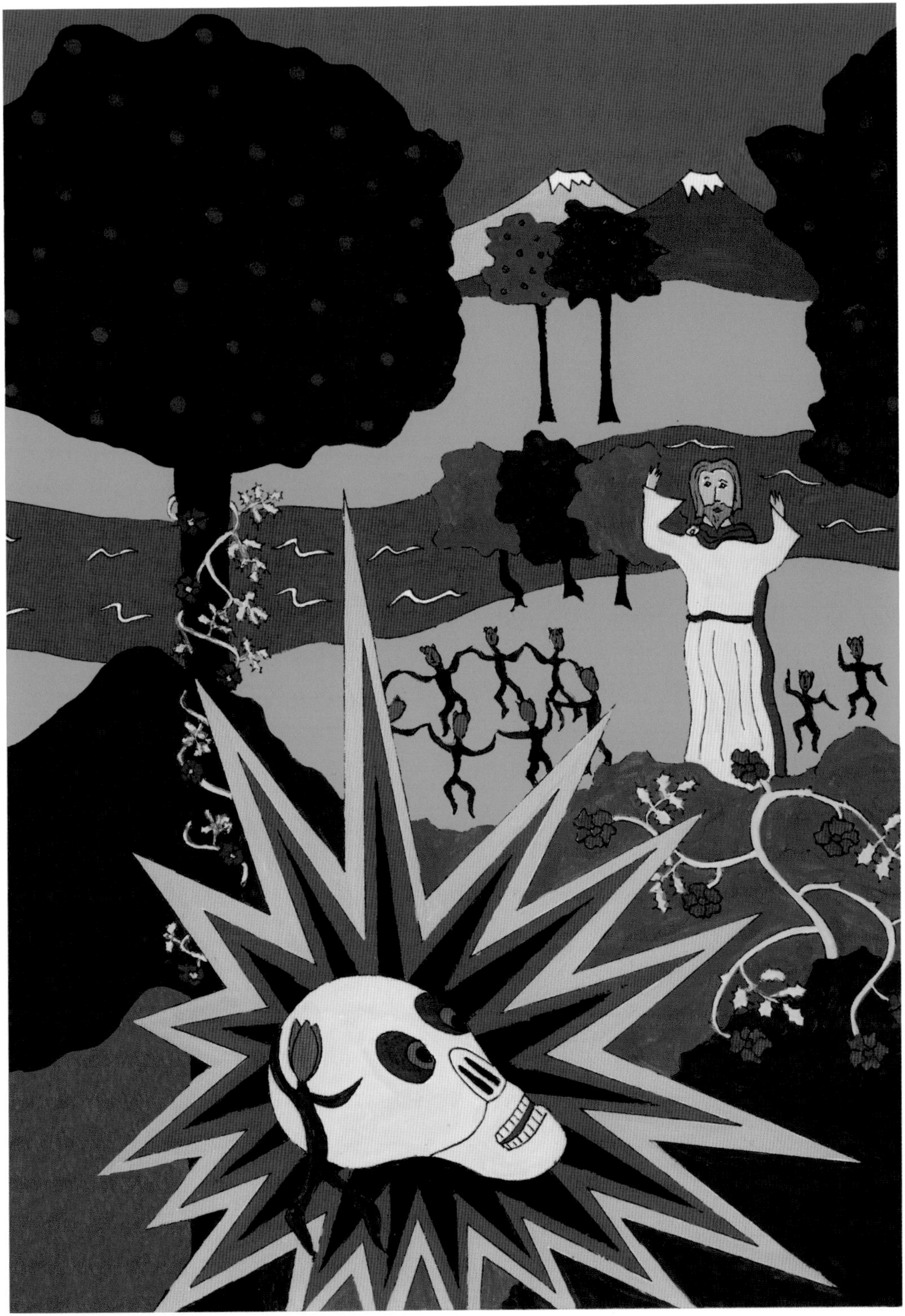

As the conditioning machine directed all the powers of evil at Boris and Tilney it began to go into reverse. The swarms of floating skulls floated back to their bodies. Suddenly the doors to the vault flew open. Charlie and Griselda screamed in horror as the skulls which Charlie had sold in the market streamed through the doors. Each skull flew to its body (except Boris who was imprisoned in the conditioning machine). As the precious plants spread in Boris's vision, the bodies in the vault began to stir. Flesh began to return to the skulls. Marks of evil disappeared. The bodies came back to life, to dance and sing.

As Boris found himself in the Garden where plants grew wild and free, there was a blinding flash of golden light. Griselda fell senseless to the ground, and all the bodies, men, women and children, flew up the stairs out into the sunlight where, passing through space and time, they returned to their loved ones, just as they had been before capture by Charlie Stench.

Only the lifeless body of Boris was left in the vault. Charlie cradled it in his arms. "All my collection gone. Years of collecting. Nothing left except the body of Boris. Boris will never get it!" he screamed, as he lifted the body on his back, and disappeared through a secret door.

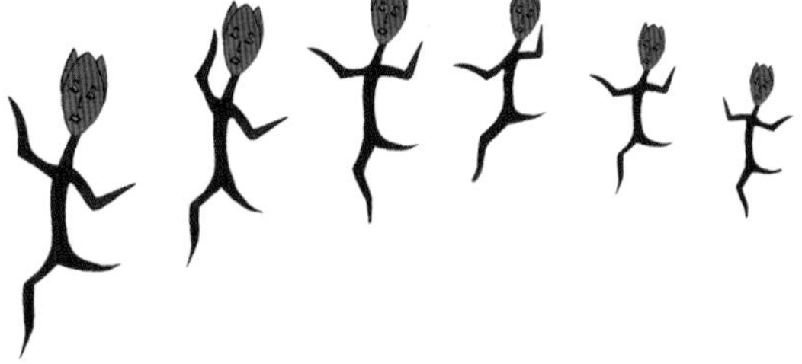

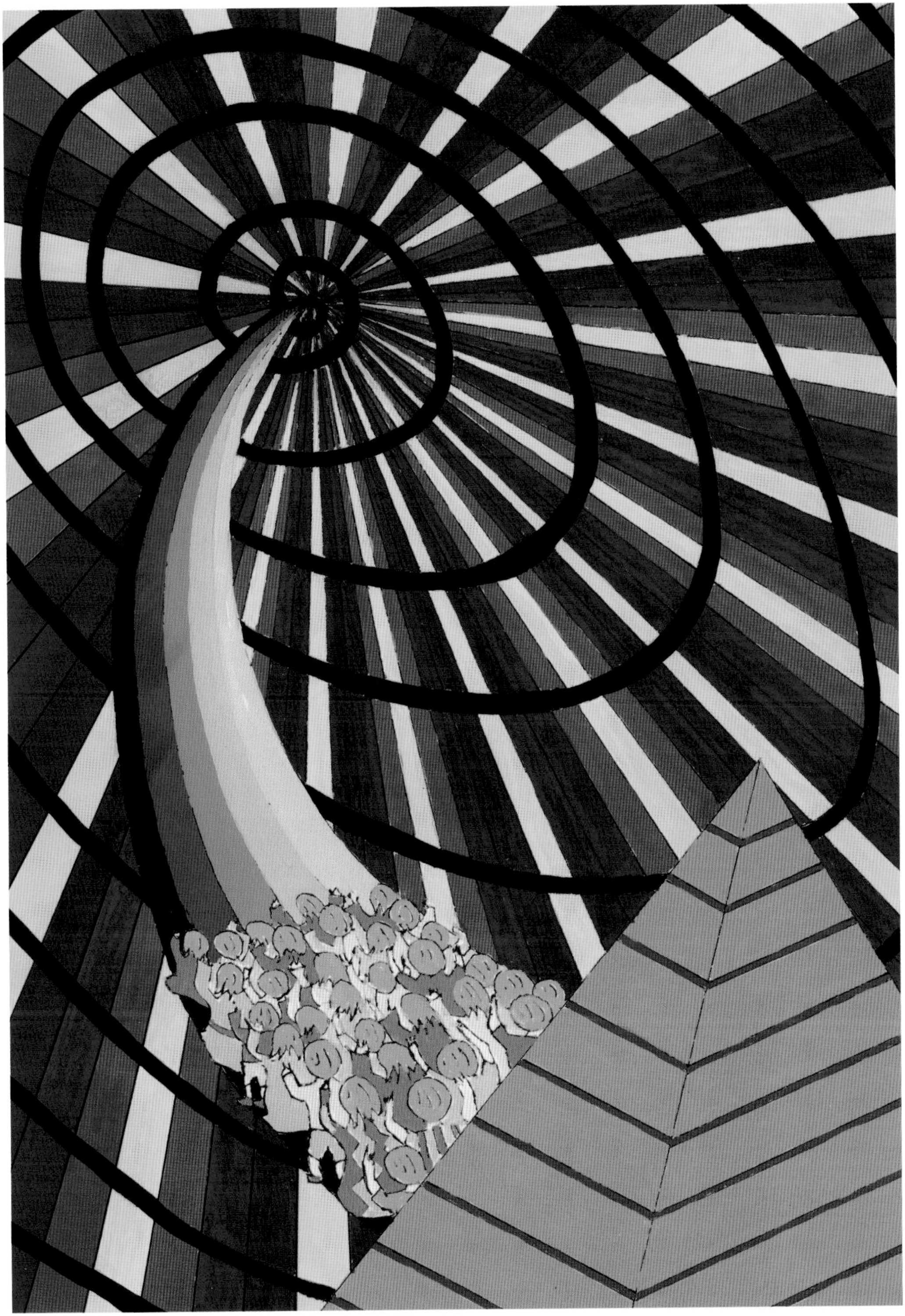

Swiftly Snuggle opened the door of the reconditioning machine. Tilney bowed, and jumped out straight into the bag around Snuggle's neck. Julius and Alex gave Benjamin a hug and they all hurried up the stairs and out into the fresh air.

When Griselda came to her senses the vault was completely deserted. "That useless skull!" gasped Griselda as she looked into the reconditioning machine. Boris was lying lifeless on the floor. He did not move. She scooped him up, popped him in a carrier bag, turned, ran up the steps, across the garden and into the forest.

The journey back to the ruined tower was much quieter than the outward journey: no whistling, no lunatic skull pretending to be a bird or plane. Griselda strode through the forest, swinging the carrier bag backwards and forwards, murmuring, "I hope that now he is evil he will fry whoever I want!" Strangely with the golden flash she had forgotten everything that had happened after Boris was put in the conditioning machine.

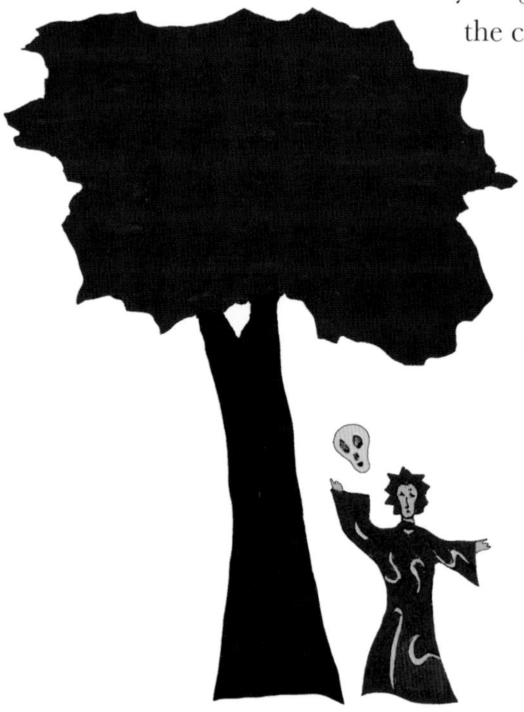

Slowly Boris began to recover, until at last he floated out of the carrier bag and asked Griselda, "What happened to me?"

"You fainted. It must have been the sight of your aged decrepit body."

"So I'm better off the way I am."

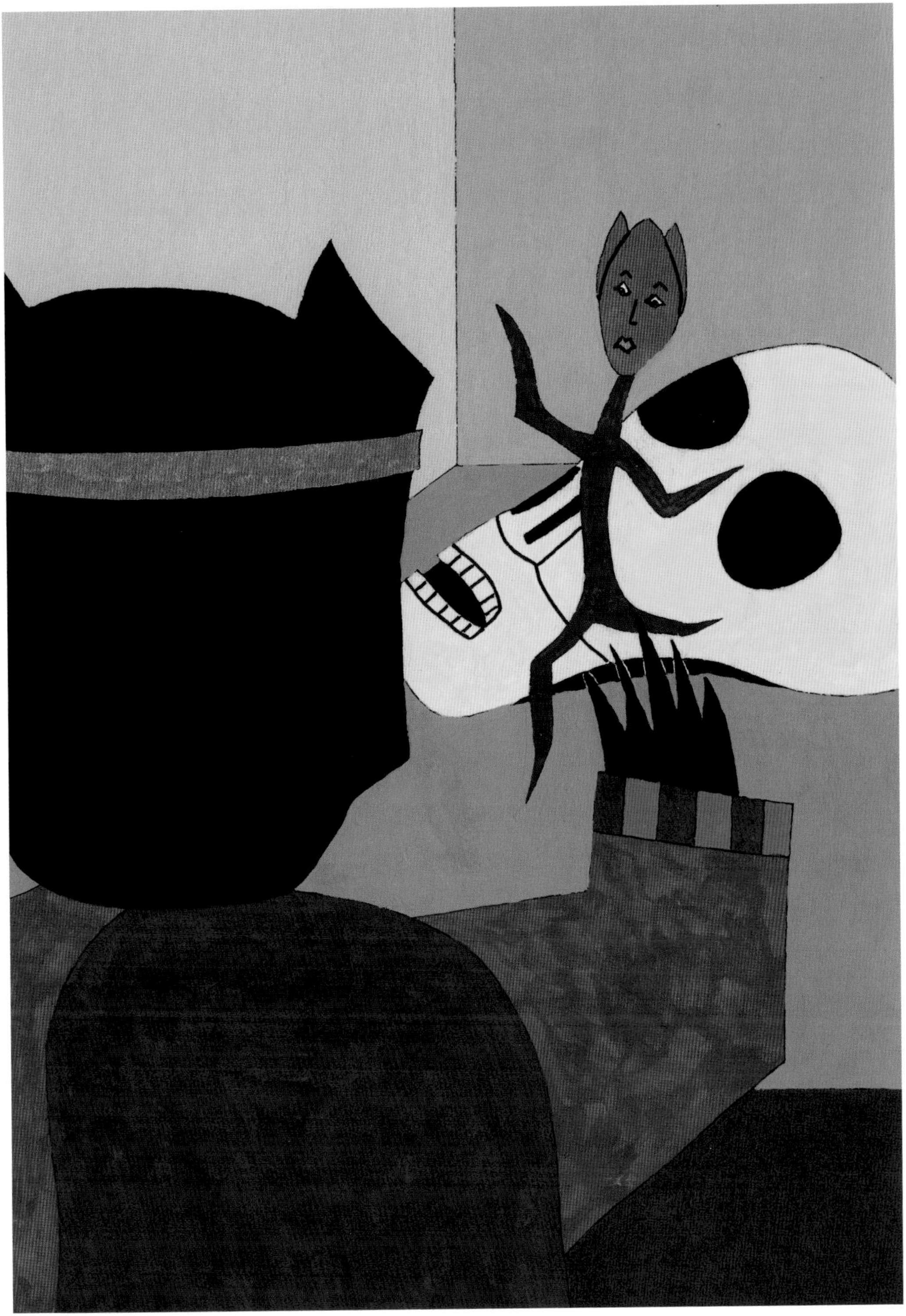

"Much, much better. I would have had no use for you if you had a body. A witch needs a skull. To fry people," she added softly.

"But, mistress, I've never fried anyone." Griselda did not answer. "Mistress, can I float upon your shoulder? I'm feeling weak. I do not know what has come over me."

"Of course, Boris. Now that you have become evil we can be friends."

"Evil? Me become evil. Are you sure?"

"Very sure, Boris. Very sure indeed."

As Griselda and Boris drew nearer to the ruined tower it began to get dark. Passing between two large oaks they came upon the boys' mother and father, anxiously looking for their children. Griselda turned her head to Boris (who was still on her shoulder). "Fry them, Boris. No silly tricks. Use your laser beams. Fry them to bits."

Boris floated from Griselda, and soaring into the air suddenly thought, "Being a skull is not so bad after all!" His eyes began to flash and sparkle, and feeling a sudden sense of fun, he shot beams of light out of his eye sockets up into the night sky in a brilliant laser show. Lower down the hillside beneath the arching light walked the boys, Snuggle (once more in the form of a cat) at their head leading them home. The boys clapped their hands and shouted their approval. But not Griselda. She was in a fury.

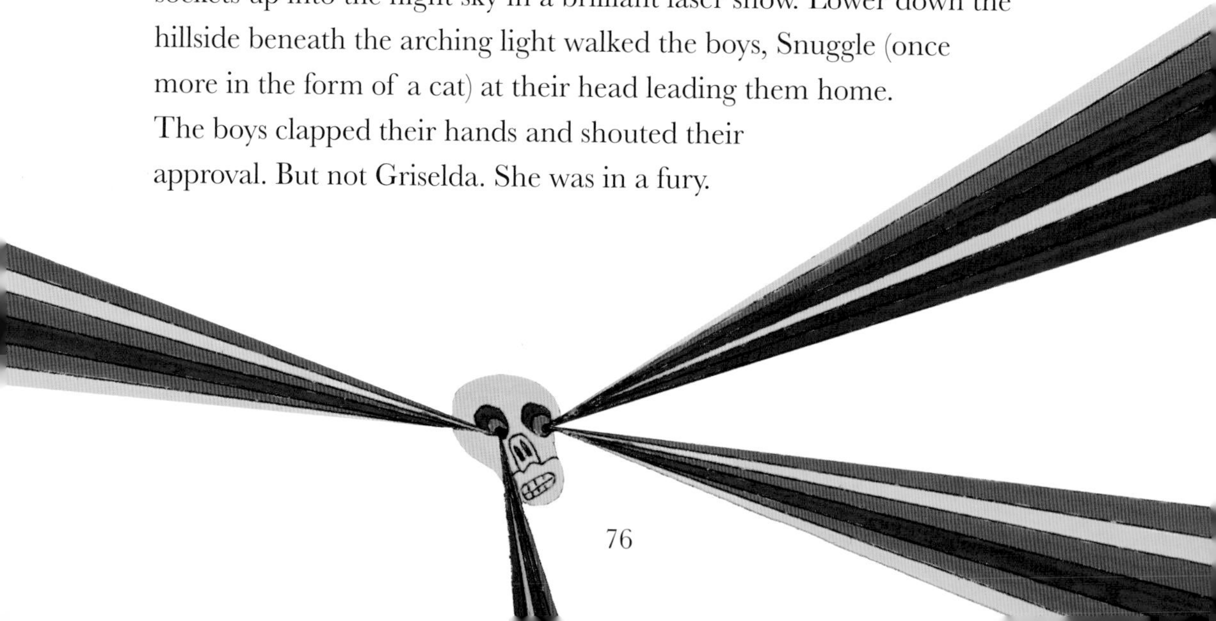

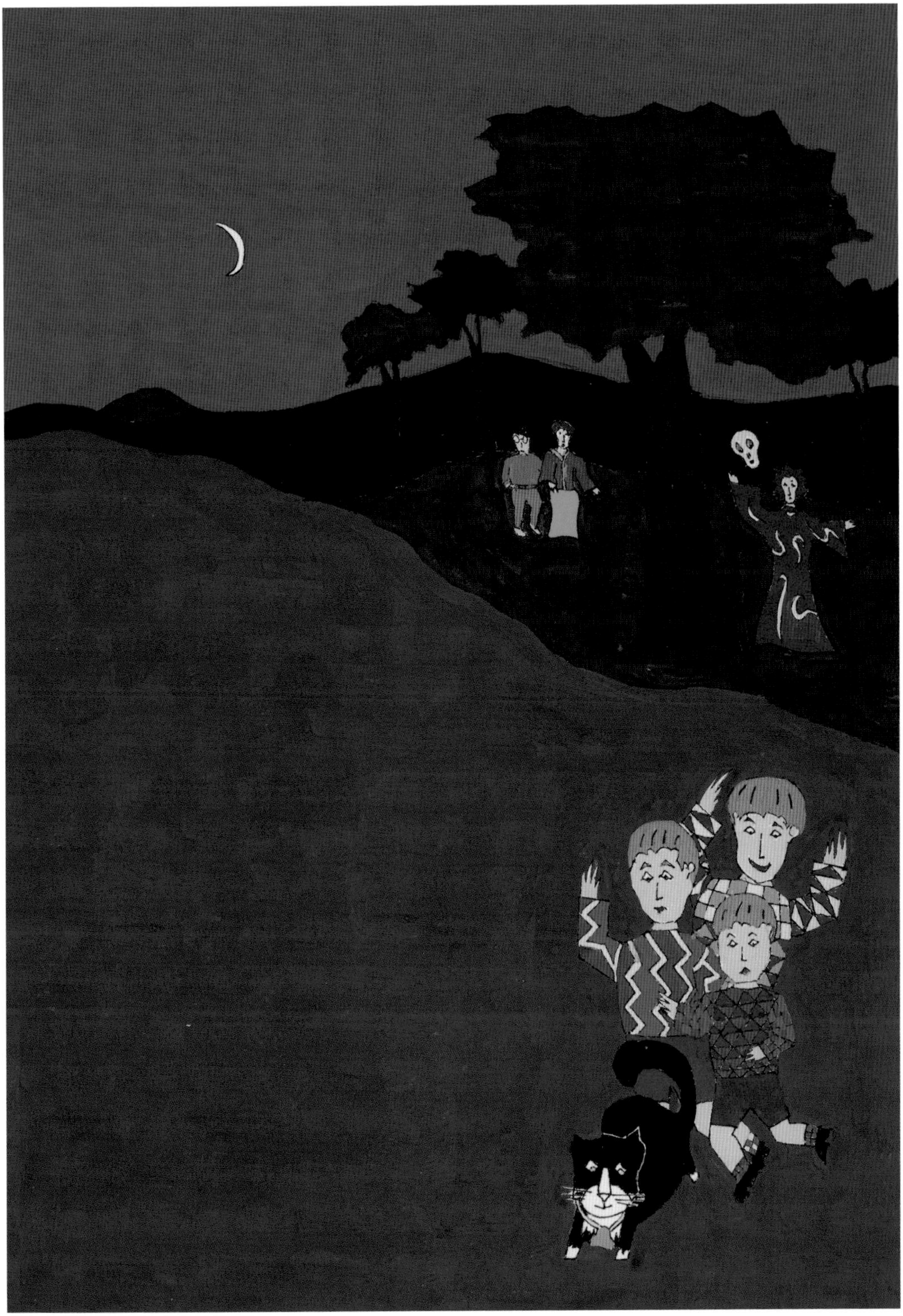

"Boris, you are useless. You have not changed at all!" Griselda screeched as she grabbed the skull, put him inside the carrier bag, spun the bag around her head and threw him far into the air.

As Boris flew through the air the bag fell from him. "This is fun!" he cried as, eyes still flashing and sparkling, he sent beams of light dancing across the sky.

"Fantastic, Boris! Brilliant!" exclaimed the boys.

Catching sight of their children the boys' mother and father ran down the hillside to join them. Their father took Benjamin into his arms and hugged him. Benjamin whispered quietly, "Sorry about the supersoaker."

"Julius! Alexander! Benjamin! What have you been up to?" demanded their mother. "We were worried."

"You shouldn't worry about us, Mum. Snuggle has been looking after us."

"Where is that cat?"

But Snuggle had crept away. He was returning Tilney to the Gardener.

78

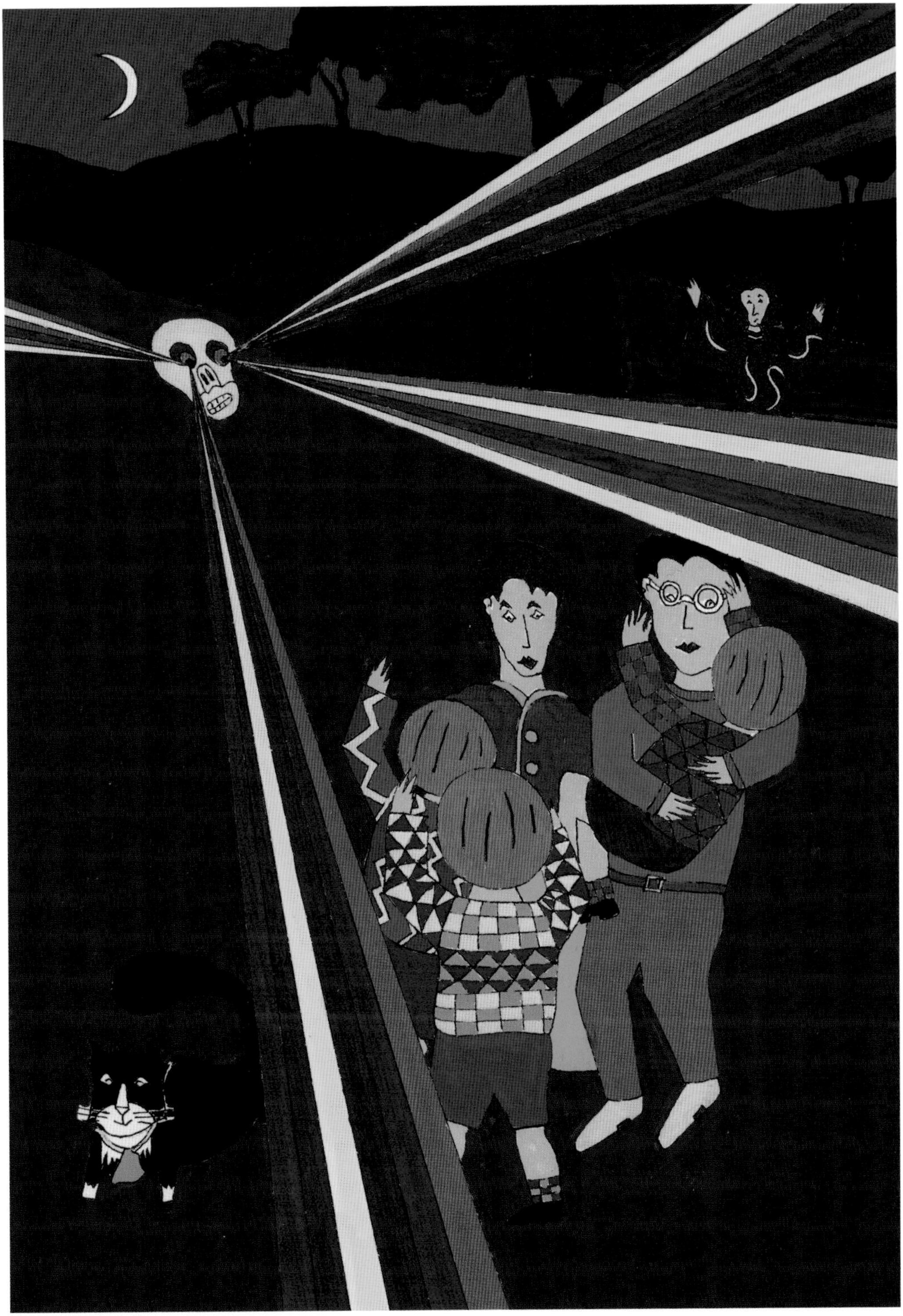

TALES OF RAMION
FACT AND FANTASY

O nce upon a time not so long ago there lived in The Old Vicarage, Shoreham, Kent (a village south of London) three boys (Julius, Alexander and Benjamin) with their mother, father and Snuggle, the misnamed family cat who savaged dogs and had a weakness for the vicar's chickens. At birthdays there were magic shows with Scrooey-Looey, a glove puppet with great red mouth who was always rude.

The boys with Snuggle

J ulius was a demanding child. Each night he wanted a different story. But he would help his father. "Dad tonight I want a story about the witch Griselda" (who had purple hair like his artist mother) "and the rabbit Scrooey-Looey and it starts like this…" His father then had to take over the story not knowing where it was going (save that the witch was not allowed to eat the children). Out of such stories grew the Tales of Ramion which were enacted with the boys' mother as Griselda and the boys' friends as Griselda's guards, the Dim Daft Dwarves (a role which came naturally to children).